LADY PEAR'S DUKE

LADY PEAR'S DUKE

BLUESTOCKINGS DEFYING ROGUES
BOOK NINE

DAWN BROWER

Journey's end in lover's meeting...

— SHAKESPEARE, TWELFTH NIGHT

CONTENTS

EXCERPT: THE VIXEN IN RED
Dawn Brower

EXCERPT: NEVER DEFY A VIXEN
Dawn Brower

EXCERPT: WHEN AN EARL
TURNS WICKED
Dawn Brower

Lady Pearyn Treedale has been affianced to Cameron Spencer, the Duke of Partridgdon since she was eight years old. An archaic practice, but a situation she's come to enjoy. At her formal introduction to society she wasn't like the other debutantes. While they all searched for husbands, she made friends, had titillating conversations, and did whatever pleased her. Her fiancé had the good grace to be absent most of her life. Then, the duke went on his world tour, and decided never to return to England, allowing Lady Pear a freedom most ladies never experience.

Now at five and twenty, Lady Pear wonders if perhaps she had it all wrong. She has friends, but no love, and no family. With Christmas around the corner, she receives gifts from a secret admirer, and she begins to believe that perhaps she should give this new gentleman her attention, because her duke certainly doesn't want her.

To love, and be loved, is the greatest gift of all. Whether that be romantic, familial, or friendship. Cherish the gifts in your life, as I intend to cherish mine. My children are the greatest loves of my life, and my purpose. Embrace yours...

CHAPTER 1

*C*ameron Spencer, the Duke of Partridgdon, stared at the fire burning in the hearth. He'd been back in London for a sennight, and the cold had already started to seep into his bones. He had been away, save for a few quick visits, from England since he turned eight and ten, three years after his father forced him to agree to betroth himself to Lady Pearyn Treedale.

He'd hated every second of it—the betrothal had controlled his life from the moment it had been signed. Traveling had been his last chance to experience freedom, until even that had seemed like a noose around his neck. If only his father had not needed the money that came with that contract...

As part of the betrothal agreement part of his

fiancée's dowry had been given to the dukedom in advance. It was the only way to save their estates, and he'd sold his son to the highest bidder. His father had used the money to build their estate, and by the time he died it was flush. The need for his bride-to-be's funds was no longer a necessity, but Cameron's fate had already been set. He may have had to agree to marry her, but that didn't mean he had to rush to the altar and officially make her his wife.

Lady Pearyn had been eight years old when the contracts had been signed. He was seven years her senior. So when he turned ten and eight, she was only eleven. It made sense to him, and to his father, when he made his case for him to skip Oxford and instead take a world tour. When his betrothed reached majority, he was expected to return, but Cameron hadn't. His father died before then and he didn't see any reason to honor that promise, at least not yet.

Cameron returned for his father's funeral when he reached one and twenty, and then promptly left again, leaving his estates in the hands of his stewards. They were thriving, and they sent him quarterly reports so he could keep tabs on his estate, from a distance. That was all he needed.

Occasionally he had to return for some business matter or the other, but he only stayed long enough to handle it, then would leave once again.

It worked for him...

He never stopped to consider how it might work for Lady Pearyn. He was now two years past his thirtieth year, and perhaps, it might be time to honor that contract. If she would still have him. They barely knew a thing about each other. She'd been a child the last time he'd spent any time with her. She hadn't broken the betrothal... Perhaps she had grown to like the idea of being a duchess one day.

Cameron ran his fingers through his hair and sighed. He couldn't discern what direction he should take. Nothing made sense to him anymore. He was home, for good, and he had to make a decision.

"Pardon me, your grace," Alfred, his butler said. Alfred had been with his family since Cameron was a boy, and he'd aged a lot in the years he'd been away. Still, he managed to move quieter than anyone Cameron had ever known.

"What is it?" he asked.

"You have a guest," Alfred informed him.

No one should know he was back in London. Who could possibly have decided to make an abrupt appearance? "Send them away," he ordered. The last thing he wanted to deal with was unwanted company. "I'm not at home to anyone." His mood darkened with each passing moment. He was not fit to be around anyone.

"You look home to me," Collin Evans, the Earl of Frossly said as he strolled into Cameron's study. "And say what you will, I'm not going anywhere. It's been months since you were last here. You didn't even come home for my wedding."

Cameron frowned. "Sorry about that." Collin was his oldest and dearest friend, but he couldn't attend that wedding. "I told you I wouldn't be there in my last letter to you. You know why it wasn't possible." He crossed the room and took the top off the decanter of brandy, then poured two fingers into a glass. Cameron held up a glass and asked, "Do you want some."

"I assume you've decided to allow me to stay then," Collin replied. "So yes, I'll have a drink with you." His golden red hair was a little disheveled. That was unlike the earl. Collin took the glass Cameron offered him and took a big swig. "I am glad you're home." He tilted his glass toward him. "Are you going to stay this time?"

Cameron rubbed his fingers around the rim of his glass. He hadn't wanted the drink, but it seemed as if it was something he should do with Collin sitting in his study. He didn't meet his friend's gaze as he said, "I'm considering it."

"You are?" There was a hint of surprise in Collin's tone. "You're not saying that to get my hopes up only to dash them."

"You've been fine without me all these years." He lifted his head and gave Collin a half smile. Cameron had ensured he remained alone without any distractions. There were no family obligations or want-to-be brides to hang over his head. Except they were always still there, no matter what. He couldn't forget about what was expected of him. He'd tried, but it never left. "You've even managed to find someone to love. I'm glad you're happy."

"I am," Collin said. "Happy that is. But you're not and haven't been for a very long time. It's rare you smile. I don't think you've known true joy since we were at Eton."

"Before I realized my family was on the brink of losing everything…" He closed his eyes and sighed. "Nothing has been close to ideal in years. I'm not sure I know how to be happy."

His parents had not been the best example. Their marriage had been contracted and had not seen any reason not to broker their son. He'd been running from his problems for too long. Avoiding home had seemed like the best thing for everyone. Maybe he'd been wrong.

Collin finished his brandy and set his glass down. Concern poured from his blue eyes. "When we were younger, at Eton, a lot of our schoolmates called you the golden boy." He gestured toward Cameron. "And not because of the color of your hair, but even that is a fair assessment I suppose. No, it was because you would one day be a duke, and they believed you had it all."

Cameron snorted. "Shows how little they knew." He did not have a golden life. His father was distant at best, and his mother rarely stayed home long enough to nod in his direction. The title meant more to her than the one child she managed to give birth to. By society's rules she owed his father a spare, but she'd said on more than one occasion he was lucky she bore him an heir. There was no love between them. That was one of the reason Cameron had avoided Lady Pearyn for so many years. He didn't want to have a marriage like the one his parents had. He wanted more, much, much more than that.

"I realize that," he said in a solemn tone. "Because I was privy to your deepest, darkest secrets." Collin leaned forward. "But this is what I want you to consider. You're not as dark as you believe yourself to be. You're good at brooding, and you can give in to fits of anger like no one I know, but where it counts, your heart is in the right place."

"None of that matters." He couldn't do anything with the hand fate had dealt him. He either accepted it or kept running. "And it does little to help me now."

"That's where you're wrong. I've met your fiancée, and she's not who you think she is. I think, if you had a conversation with her, you would realize that perhaps you both want the same thing. She's had to live in your shadow as much as you've lived in hers. It's time to do something other than take the next ship across the channel. Stay and face your past, and then, move forward into a future of your own making."

Cameron sipped his brandy. Collin had given him a lot to consider, but he wasn't as convinced as he was that Lady Pearyn wanted the same thing he did. "How do you know what she wants? Has she told you?"

"Not in so many words," Collin admitted. "She puts on a brave face for the world. She throws parties and endorses artists of all kinds. Her salon is always full, and there are always men there ready and willing to gain her attention. She flirts and laughs, but it never quite reaches her eyes. I think she's lonely. As long as you have a tether on her she cannot move forward any more than you can. She's not happy either. Don't you think you owe it to her to set her free if you're not going to stake your claim?"

There was a lot in his friend's words for him to absorb. Was Lady Pearyn truly unhappy? He had selfishly considered her as title hungry as her parents and never once thought she might want something more. He'd kept his distance and hadn't taken the time to learn more about her. Cameron had not even bothered to write her. He had spied on her from a distance and she'd appeared happy, and he'd assumed she was fine. Had he been wrong?

"You may be right," Cameron began. "But I don't know where to begin." Should he pay a call on her? Write her? "We may be betrothed, but we're not... familiar with each other."

"There is that." Collin snickered. "I am not certain she even knows what you look like. Though I cannot say the same for you. There was that one instance in the park in the spring. How do you know her appearance but she doesn't have the same privilege?"

It was confession time. "I may have sneaked a glance at her a few times over the years." His curiosity had gotten the best of him. Cameron had wanted to know what she looked like. She'd grown into a beauty, but a part of him had feared his parents would have attached him to a plain woman or worse. They had only cared about the money after all. "It was easy enough on the few times that I traveled back, after my father's death. I needed to know…"

"If you might find her favorable?" Collin asked. "And do you?"

Lady Pearyn was one of the most stunning women Cameron had the privilege of laying his eyes upon. Her hair was as dark as the night sky and her eyes were a pure blue so lovely he could easily become lost in them. He never got close enough to get a true glimpse of their exquisiteness though. That would mean announcing his presence, something he was loath to do. "She is passable," he replied noncommittally. "So she flirts?" He tried to keep his tone casual, but he feared he failed in that endeavor. "None have caught her interest?"

"Would it matter if they had?" Collin raised a brow. "You don't truly want her, do you?"

That was the rub. He didn't know what he

wanted, but he was starting to suspect that he did indeed desire to know more about his fiancée. "And would you tell me if she decided to have an affair?"

"If you want me to. I suppose I would." Collin stood. "But until this moment I never believed you wanted to know a thing about her. If you're that curious you should come over during Christmastide, and the weeks leading up to it. My wife has invited a lot of people and it's going to be quite the crush. You have a couple weeks to decide." He took a quick breath. "I can also finally introduce you to her. She's heard a lot about my friend Cameron, but she has yet to realize who you are exactly. It'll be entertaining, to say the least."

"You would throw me to the wolves?" Cameron said shocked. "I thought you liked me."

"I do like you," Collin said. "But I love my wife. Don't make me chose." He strolled to the door. "I must go, but do let me know when you make a decision."

Cameron nodded. "If, and when, I elect to claim my fiancée, she'll be the first to know." He met his friend's gaze. "But you'll be a close second. For now, I'll have to decline your generous invitation, and give my best to your wife."

Collin chuckled as he left. Cameron stared at his

brandy glass, drank the rest of it, then set the glass down next to the decanter. Perhaps Collin was right. First, he had to gather a little information and discern the best way to proceed. It was time to truly get to know his betrothed.

CHAPTER 2

Two weeks later...

*L*ady Pearyn Treedale stared out the window of her London townhouse and sighed. The windows had frosted over and cold had seeped through into the room. It didn't bother her. Nothing did anymore. She was five and twenty, and where she'd found happiness at the beginning of her launch in society, no joy seemed currently present in her life. When her parents had explained she'd been affianced to the Duke of Partridgdon—the Marquess of Woodstone at the time—at the age of eight she'd shrugged it off. Why wouldn't she have? She had been a mere girl whose greatest concern was her doll and playing in her mother's garden. What did she care about some future duke?

In society, becoming a duchess was as close to being a princess as a lady could possibly reach. Her mother was more excited for Pearyn than she could ever be, had ever been... She closed her eyes and pictured her mother the last time she'd seen her. It had been on her sickbed nearly a decade earlier. She'd been pale. Her skin almost translucent and appeared papery in texture. Cheekbones more prominent than they had ever been and eyes a dull hazel rounded out her sickened expression. She'd lost a lot of weight and was merely skin and bones.

It was hard for her to admit, but Pearyn hadn't wanted to go into her chambers. She would have preferred to remember her mother as the beautiful, vibrant woman she'd always been to her. Not a woman with stringy black hair and a bony frame. Her mother had whispered in her ear, "I don't want to die." The fear and sadness in her mother's voice had decimated her. Death was not a pretty sight, and it had undone Pearyn. Her heart had dropped and her stomach became a bundle of unease. Tears had burned in her eyes, but she managed to hold them back as she said to her mother, "I know mama. I know." No one ever wanted to die? How terrified she must have been… If Pearyn could have eased that pain in any way, she would have. She'd hugged her mother and did the best she could with the limited options left to her. Thinking about her mother, and Pearyn's impotence during that dreadful time, still had the ability to break her heart.

Those moments would come to haunt her forever. Her mother's last words and the way she'd looked that day. She'd died alone, without any family with her. Pearyn should have stayed, but her mother had told her to go. It was no way to spend the last moments of a person's life. Pearyn's father, the Earl of Beaumont, hadn't bothered to look in on his wife at all. He had his heir, and his daughter would one day be a duchess. His countess had done her duty, and he had known his…to ensure that his children fulfilled their obligations to the family line.

So it was a disappointment to the earl that Pearyn still had not said her vows and married the duke. He thought she'd done something wrong to ensure the duke had stayed away. Pearyn hadn't seen the duke since she was eight years old. She didn't even know if she'd recognize him if he stood right in front of her. All she knew with certainty was he had blond hair and green eyes. The rest…complete blank.

She had enjoyed his absence over the years. It had given her a certain amount of freedom. There was the occasional rogue who thought they could woo her into bed, but for the most part, no gentleman pursued her in truth. Her betrothal was well known, and they didn't bother trying to steal her away from having the title of duchess. They danced with her because she was safe. She shouldn't have aspirations for anything more than a spot of fun, and she'd had experienced so many amusements...

Now though, the fun had stopped. They still danced with her and doted on her because they knew her heart was not engaged. That was part of the problem. She felt nothing. Not even the slightest interest in romance or attraction. None of them interested her. Was something wrong with her? Was she as cold as the frost coating the windows? Did the duke somehow sense that, and that was why he'd stayed away?

Melancholy had become her best friend of late...

At least she could afford to live on her own. The duke didn't seem to be in a hurry to return home. Her maternal grandmother had left her a sizeable fortune and the London townhouse. Her dowry was separate from her inheritance, and hers to do as she pleased.

"Pardon me, my lady," her butler said. "There's a missive that arrived for you."

"Bring it to me," she replied. What could it possibly be?

The butler strolled over to her and held out a silver tray. On it lay a dark red folded paper sealed with a symbol she didn't recognize. It almost looked like a tree with a bird sitting on its bare branches. Pearyn frowned and plucked it off the tray. She broke the seal and pulled out a hand-painted Christmas card. It had a large pine tree with decorations on it. She flipped it open and smiled. There was no signature, but it did have a sonnet written in elegant script inside, she assumed was meant as a message to her.

> *Cold is the frigid winds of winter*
> *Frozen is the ties that bind*
> *My purpose will never splinter*
> *For it's your love I seek, and will find*
>
> *Distance has not been kind*
> *For it has kept us apart*
> *You're not far from my mind*
> *And I hope to win your heart*

With this gift my intentions are clear
Soon we will meet once more
And I'll hold you, my dear
On the night marked twenty-four

All doubts will be washed away
And love will reign on that day...

What did that mean? Who would have written this? Did this mean she'd discover their identity on Christmas Eve? Pearyn frowned and closed the card. She usually adored a good mystery, but she was weary. She didn't know how she felt about this new development. Prior to this, no gentleman had courted her because of her betrothal. Had they decided that she was free now? Did they consider the duke's absence a permanent one? What could they know that she didn't?

She had more questions than answers, and it irritated her. Perhaps she should show it to her closest friend, Charlotte. She was supposed to see her later at Lady Harrington's for tea. She'd bring the card and let all the ladies give their opinions...

CAMERON STARED AT LADY PEARYN'S TOWNHOUSE. He'd spotted her in one of the windows. She was as beautiful as he remembered. He never got too close, but he'd spied on her from a distance from time to time. More so in the past fortnight as he contemplated what his next move should be. The more he learned about her, the more he wanted to know her in truth. He had to play it right and engage her mind and keep her interest.

It was bloody cold out though, and he couldn't stand outside her townhouse much longer. He had an engagement he had to see to. His possible pursuit of his lady could wait. She'd waited this long, and he assumed she'd wait a little longer for him to discern what was best. Hopefully, she didn't hit him over the head when they finally were in the same room together.

Cameron walked away from the prominent Mayfair townhouses and hailed a hackney that was nearby. He should have ridden his horse, at least. What had he been thinking? When the hackney stopped, he told the driver where he was heading and slid inside. Hopefully, it wouldn't take long to reach Harrington's club. Cameron wasn't a member, but he wanted to meet with the Earl of Harrington and the Earl of Shelby. Collin wasn't in London at the moment and wouldn't return for another week or so. Possibly longer depending on the weather.

The hackney came to a stop outside a nondescript house. There was nothing remarkable about it, and that as probably how Harrington and his cohorts preferred it. Cameron paid the driver and strolled up to the door. He rapped on it several times until it swung open. A man with dark blond hair and deep blue eyes stood on the other side. "Yes?" he asked.

"I'm here to see Harrington."

He stepped aside and let him enter. "Wait here. Who should I tell him is calling?"

"I'm the Duke of Partridgdon," he said simply. Sometimes Cameron hated the title. It changed how people treated him once he introduced himself. This man didn't seem to care one iota though. He just nodded and walked away. There was not 'your graces' spilling from his mouth. It was...refreshing.

Cameron stared at a mirror that had been hung near a coat rack. It was oval and filled most of the wall floor to ceiling. It was an odd piece of decoration, and he couldn't help wondering why they'd chosen it. The only thing a person would see was themselves when they entered. Was this a reminder of some sort, and if so, of what? He didn't want to over-analyze the mirror. It might just simply be a mirror with no ulterior design.

"Partridgdon?" Harrington said as he strolled into the foyer. "What brings you to London?" No, why are you at my club. No, he'd always been welcome at the club, it was England he'd never believed he belonged. "And not even when we have anything remotely resembling nice weather. I thought you'd decided to stay away forever."

"You know how it is…" He shrugged. "The heart grows weary of being away from home. I had to return at some juncture."

Harrington grinned and brushed a dark lock of hair off his forehead. "Follow me. You look like you could use a drink or several."

Cameron fell into step behind the earl as he led him down a long hall and into a far room. His office, Cameron assumed. It was outlined in dark colors. Rich mahogany leather chairs and dark purple curtains covered the windows. His desk was dark and solid with little embellishments to it. The room suited Harrington.

Harrington lifted a decanter off of a shelf and two glasses. He set them on his desk and poured two fingers of brandy into each, then handed one to Cameron. "Have a seat and enjoy."

Cameron took the glass and sat. He sipped the brandy, and it burned as it traveled down his throat. It warmed and soothed at the same time. Harrington had been right. He had needed this. "Thank you."

"You're welcome," Harrington said. "Now perhaps you are ready to tell me why you are here."

"I need your help." There was no other way to say it. If he hoped to have any chance with Lady Pearyn, he had to do it right, and he needed a way in. He hoped to woo her without her realizing who he was. Maybe it was the cowardly way, but he felt he needed to do it this way. He had to know if she wanted him or his title.

"What do you need?" Harrington said simply.

Cameron grinned. This was why he'd come to Harrington. He'd gotten to know him and the Earl of Shelby through Collin. Both men had married into Collin's family. They were far more reliable than Cameron's family had ever been, and since his father had died, he didn't have anyone to rely on anyway. "I've decided it is time to claim my bride."

"It's about damn time," Harrington replied. There was a bit of amusement in his tone. "Why now?"

He shrugged. "I've stayed away long enough. I want to go home, and if that means marrying Lady Pearyn Treedale...so be it." Unless he could find a way to nullify that contract... "And I would like for you to help me arrange a few meetings that seem innocuous and ordinary."

"Like a chance meeting at a ball?" Harrington lifted a brow.

"Precisely," Cameron answered. "Considering the time of year, there are not too many of those happening."

"Leave it to me," he said. "The ladies always want a reason to have some sort of social gathering. Expect some invitations."

"I appreciate it." Cameron finished his brandy and stood. "Now I have other arrangements to make." He nodded at Harrington. "Until we see each other again." With those words he exited the office, then the club, and returned home. He had many plans to devise and a lady to pursue.

CHAPTER 3

*T*he sun had started to set, and with the disappearance of its welcoming light, a gloom had settled in the sitting room of Pearyn's townhouse. Perhaps it was her mood more than anything. Lately she'd been on the edge of melancholy and nothing seemed to shake it. The only speck of brightness she'd experienced was receiving that card the day before. It had intrigued her and gave her a reason to keep her tea appointment with her friends. That hadn't lasted long. She'd gone home and once again given into her despondent feelings, and retired early for the evening.

She didn't have that luxury today. Lady Helena, the Marchioness of Dashville, had sent her an invitation to join them for dinner, and she had foolishly accepted. How could she be so darned lonely even amongst her closest friends? Would her despair ever shake loose and give her something more to latch on to?

Pearyn shook her dismal thoughts away. It was the time of year, nothing more. Christmas would be in two short weeks and after it was over the reminder of her mother's passing would fade away, at least for a little while. It was harder during the holidays. The reminder kept itself in the forefront of her mind and wouldn't let go.

"My lady," her butler said as he entered the room. "My apologies. I know you wished to remain undisturbed, but a package arrived for you."

She lifted a brow. "It's for me?" Usually packages were delivered to the kitchen because they were meant for the household, not Pearyn personally. It had been quite a while since she had done any shopping for herself. She probably would benefit from a visit to the modiste, but she didn't believe in spending money unnecessarily. Perhaps instead she'd send a missive to her favorite seamstress instead. She was more frugal than the modiste and had a fresh eye for new designs. She tilted her head to the side and asked, "Are you certain?"

"I am, my lady," the butler said. "It was delivered through the kitchen as all our packages are, but it has got a note on it addressed to you."

How odd…first the card and now this. Pearyn took the package from her butler and carried it over to the settee. She sat down and lifted the note from the package and read it.

Sweets, for my sweet Pear. May they tantalize your tongue and lead to thoughts of me…

—Eternally Yours

IT WAS UNSIGNED LIKE THE CARD HAD BEEN. WHO WAS sending her these gifts? The note suggested they were candy of some sort. Pearyn didn't like sweets as a rule, but she did indulge every so often. She tore off the paper over the box, then lifted the lid. Inside were several sugared almond bon bons wrapped in colored tissue paper. She smiled and tore away the tissue paper on one and then popped it into her mouth. Pearyn sighed with pleasure as the sweetness hit her tongue. Perhaps this was exactly what she had needed.

She ate two more candies, then reluctantly placed

the lid back on the box, and set it on the table next to the settee. Pearyn didn't have a lot of time to dawdle eating sweets. She had to prepare for the dinner party at the Dashville's. Pearyn sighed and stood, then brushed her skirts with her hands. She'd tell a maid to give the sweets to the servants. She'd indulged enough, and she didn't feel as if she could fully appreciate something when others didn't have the same privilege. It was a nice surprise to receive, and she did enjoy them.

Pearyn strolled out of the sitting room and headed up to her room. She'd have a bath and then have her maid help her dress for the evening. Her spirits were better, and she wanted to look as pretty as she could manage. It helped her to feel pretty when she was out. It might be vain of her, but there really was nothing like a beautiful gown and a lovely hairstyle to help her feel wonderful.

She whistled as she entered her chamber. Beatrice, her lady's maid, was already there waiting for her. "My lady," she greeted. "I have pressed your lavender gown for the evening."

"Perfect," Pearyn replied. "Draw me a bath. There is a box of bon bons in my sitting room. When we're finished, please take them to share with the other maids."

"Of course, my lady." Beatrice did as Pearyn directed. Once she was settled in her bath, the maid left her to finish bathing. She would return when it was time for Pearyn to dress.

For the first time all day, Pearyn was looking forward to the dinner party. She had a feeling it would be far better than she anticipated. Of course she might be wrong, but at least she was no longer feeling a bit of the doldrums.

Cameron had been invited to dinner, but he'd skipped the main course. He didn't want to sit next to his betrothed and make small talk. His desire was to catch her where she least expected him. A moment in time that would be in secret and they could share something much more intimate. He didn't want any witnesses or introductions. There was a time and place for such things, and it wasn't at a dinner table. He appreciated the marchioness for inviting him. It gave him access to her home, and a way to have his first real meeting with Lady Pearyn.

He had stood outside as all the guests arrived. It had not been a small gathering, which also helped his cause. Once everyone was inside and settled in for the meal, Cameron had gone inside. The servants were all bustling around to serve the guests, and no one stopped to question him. He had his invitation in his inside pocket on the off chance they did. He'd been to Dashville's town house several times in the past, so he was familiar with the layout. He went to the library to pour himself a glass of brandy. If his fiancée was true to form she'd sneak away at some juncture and come here.

Cameron had studied her over the years. Not in person, and not up close, but he'd learned enough to know what she was drawn to. She loved books, history, poetry, and art. This library had all of that. She may have already been inside the room before, but she'd still gravitate toward it. Lady Pearyn might like to pretend she was unpredictable, but she wasn't.

He went to the bar set up near the desk and poured a glass of brandy, then carried it over to the settee near the window. It was dark in the library. Cameron hadn't bothered to light any candles. The only light in the room came from the moon's illumination. Would she light a candle when she came in? That much he didn't know. His information was limited, and that was why he was using so much subterfuge. Cameron hoped he didn't overplay his hand with all his scheming.

With a sigh, he stepped away from the window and sat on a chair in the cover of darkness and waited. Dinner should be over and the ladies would retire to one room, and the gentleman to another. At least for a little while until they all came together for some sort of entertainment. Cameron wouldn't be a part of any of it, and he hoped his assumptions about Lady Pearyn were right, and she too would not take part in the societal norms.

He didn't have long to wait. The door slid open, and a woman entered, then went right to the window. The moonlight illuminated her beauty and made her appear almost ethereal. Her dark hair was twisted into an elegant chignon with a few dark tendrils floating over her alabaster skin. Her cheekbones were prominent and her lips were a perfect bow shape, and a dusty pink, like a rose at first bloom. He'd known she was beautiful, but this close, she was breathtaking. Cameron was momentarily stunned. He glanced down at her lavender gown. It was simple and elegant and hugged her curves nicely. Her pert breasts were outlined in silk and chiffon. They tempted him, something he hadn't counted on.

Cameron stood and took a few steps toward her. In a husky tone he asked, "Hoping for a wishing star?" It was silly, but he hoped it was enough to entice her into a conversation with a stranger.

She turned toward him and squinted. "Do you always skulk in dark corners?" He could almost hear the smile in her voice as she spoke. Cameron had amused her...he considered that a good sign to proceed with his plan.

He chuckled softly. "Not always. Only when it is more appealing than a crowd of sycophants." That was perhaps too acerbic a description of the dinner guests. He *did* have friends at the dinner party after all, but he had come for other reasons.

"That's a tad harsh," Lady Pearyn said, as she narrowed her gaze, again, in an attempt to study him. "Why come at all if you feel that way about your hosts?" There was a lightness in her tone mixed with a longing. Cameron wanted to uncover the depths of that desire, to unravel the mystery of Lady Pearyn Treedale.

"Oh," he began. "It's not them I consider unworthy. There are several individuals here I consider friends. It's the rest of them I cannot abide."

So far she seemed congenial as she conversed with him. Too bad he couldn't trust she would want more from him if she were aware of his true identity.

"I suppose there is truth in that." She agreed, of course, otherwise she wouldn't be in the library with him. He didn't say that to her, though. "But you could at least have tolerated them through dinner."

"Like you did?" He took another step toward her but stayed out of the light. She could make out some of his features since he wasn't completely shrouded in darkness, but not enough to identify him. "I prefer my own company, and I wasn't hungry. This seemed more prudent, and I can converse with the marquess later."

She sighed. "I still think it was rude of you to hide in here." She tilted her head to the side. "Who are you?"

"No one of importance," he replied smoothly. He sipped his brandy and then boldly met her gaze. "You're quite lovely. Don't you have a suitor or several hoping to convince you to marry them?"

"Are you offering?" she countered. If she only knew...

Cameron grinned. "Not at all. I'm afraid marriage has never been one of my desires, and I doubt that will change." She was the only one he *would* marry, but he couldn't say that to her, at least not yet. He had to be sure of her. It might be a bit drastic, but this was his way for them to become more acquainted, and see if something more could bloom between them.

"A pity," she said. Her tone didn't suggest she was disappointed. It almost sounded...sarcastic.

"You wanted that honor," he chided her. He had to say the words. Cameron had to discern her truth one way or another.

"Not at all," she said easily. "I don't think I'll ever marry." There was a sadness in her tone.

"Why not?" he asked, unable to keep the shock out of his tone. "You prefer to be an old maid?" Cameron never would have guessed she relished the spinster lifestyle.

"No," she said. That sadness had creeped back into her voice. That one word a cold shiver down his spine. "I should have married by now. I guess I am not desirable enough, even when my father arranges a marriage of convenience, that isn't in any way...convenient."

Cameron's heart stopped at her words. He'd done this to her. His absence had made her doubt herself, and he owed her a great debt for his ignorance and selfishness. He had stayed away because he resented her, and not once had he considered her feelings. "I'm sorry."

"For what?" She snorted. "You didn't sign the contract tying me to a man who'd rather sail around the world than bother to come home and claim his unwanted bride." She sighed. "It's not your fault though, I do appreciate the sentiment."

She was wrong. It was entirely his fault. He should stop this charade now and tell her who he was. She might slap him for it, but he'd deserve it. "No woman should feel undesirable."

Cameron stepped closer to her and pulled her into his arms. "What are you doing?"

"Righting a wrong," he said simply. Cameron leaned down and pressed his lips to hers. This had not been part of his plan, but he felt helpless. He had to do something to make her realize she deserved better than, well, him...even if she had no idea he was her intended.

The kiss started soft and gentle as he coaxed her into it. When their tongues touched, it turned into a dueling match for control, one which he barely won. He took over the kiss, deepened it, and explored her mouth with an intensity he hadn't realized existed. He wanted the kiss to go on, to move to something far more intimate, but she wasn't ready, and he refused to take her before they said any vows.

He mentally cursed and pulled back. It seemed he had made a decision. Cameron wanted Lady Pearyn Treedale. Now all he had to do was convince her marrying him was the best thing for the both of them. "Don't give up on yourself," he said cryptically. "Sometimes what you want most is right in front of you, and sometimes, it takes a while for it to present itself. Have faith."

With those words he left her alone in the library. He had to revise some of his plans, and he wasn't exactly certain where he should start. One thing was clear, he desired his bride-to-be, and he was in for one hell of night after that kiss.

CHAPTER 4

*P*earyn sat at her vanity as her maid styled her hair in a simple plait, then wound around almost like a crown that rested on an angle on top her head. The gown she had chosen to wear to the theater was a light blue violet silk that matched the shade of her eyes—or so her seamstress had insisted. Pearyn had never bothered to compare them. She didn't much care if the shades were identical. The gown was gorgeous and hugged her curves and had a low décolletage, bordering on too risqué, but Pearyn didn't care. That had only added to the appeal of the dress. She might not be a married woman, but she was tired of acting the innocent debutante. There was a need deep inside of her. She wanted more, but she didn't know yet what that more consisted of. So she was taking chances she normally would not have taken. She felt...emboldened.

The two gifts she'd received had given her hope. Someone out there wanted to court her. It might be secretive, but it was still quite exciting. Maybe it was time to forget about the Duke of Partridgdon and move on with her life. She deserved more than an absentee fiancé who couldn't even be bothered to write her. She had tasted freedom at the moment when she fully entered society and held on to it as if her life had deepened upon it. Pearyn hadn't known what the cost of that freedom would entail. She never could have foreseen the loneliness that would hover around the edges of her independence. Friendship wasn't enough. At the end of the day, those dear friends returned home to their husbands and children. Pearyn remained by herself with nothing but pretty art and masterful pieces of literature, and the servants who kept their distance.

She had regrets, but there was no way for her to go back and alter the decisions she'd made, so she must move forward. To try and right the mistakes she made by ensuring she had a better future, a family, and if she was lucky enough, love.

Satisfied that she looked presentable, Pearyn rose

and turned to her maid, "Thank you," she said quietly. "Will you retrieve my wrap for me?"

"Yes, my lady," she said, and went to do as Pearyn had asked. It didn't take long for Beatrice to return. She held the wrap open for Pearyn and helped her slip it on.

"I'll be out late," Pearyn said. The theater was one of her favorite places. The Covent Garden theater had decided to do one of the Bards plays, and she looked forward to it. The Twelfth Night was a good choice so close to Christmas, and it was one of her favorites. "Don't wait up for me."

The gown she was wearing didn't require assistance in removing it. It had several tiny buttons that went up the side, and she could easily undo those herself. Pearyn had foregone wearing stays ages ago. They were a nuisance, and she preferred breathing. Besides, she had a slender frame that didn't need the extra support that stays would provide.

"Very well, my lady," Beatrice replied. "Enjoy the theater."

"I intend to." Pearyn replied. "Lady Asthey, Lady Shelby, and Lady Harrington are going to join me. It should be quite pleasant." It would be better if her closest friend, Charlotte, Lady Frossly, could join her, but the three countesses that were attending with her were quite amiable. Lady Asthey was Charlotte's sister-in-law, and she could deliver news regarding her friend. Charlotte was still at her husband's family estate, but should be returning to town soon. Pearyn missed her dearly.

Pearyn left her chambers and went down the stairs. Her butler stood in the foyer waiting for her. "Good evening, my lady," he said and bowed. "Your carriage awaits you outside."

She pasted a smile on her face and nodded. "Enjoy your evening, Albert," she said. "Have Mrs. Simmons make you all something special. Maybe some chocolate to sit by the fire with."

"Very well, my lady." He opened the door for her. "Your generosity is too much, but the staff will enjoy it."

"I hope they do." She slid her gloves on as she exited the house. The bitter cold stung her cheeks. She took a deep breath. The icy air cooled the warmth inside her mouth, leaving a frozen path in its wake. It was worse when she breathed through her nose. At least it wasn't snowing…

A footman opened the door to the carriage and assisted her inside. During warmer months Pearyn liked to walk when she could, depending on her destination. In the winter she tried to stay at home as much as possible. She hated snow and freezing wind. She much preferred to bury herself under her quilts on her bed and sleep as long as possible. Unfortunately, she wasn't allowed to do such things as much as she wanted to.

The carriage rolled down the road, and they were off to the theater. She couldn't wait to be inside the walls of the Covent Garden theater. The play would give her a little bit of time to forget her loneliness and become lost in the story the actors presented. The pit would be filled with people that talked too loud and paid little attention to the play itself. Even some of the boxes would be like that. Pearyn was one of the few individuals that attended the theater that actually went for the entertainment the actors provided.

She had been lost in her own thoughts as the carriage rattled along the icy streets. So it was a welcome surprise when she realized that the theater was in sight. The carriage came to a stop near the front of the theater. Pearyn rapped on the carriage. "I'll get out here and walk the rest of the way." There was a line of carriages in front of her and she had a need to escape the confines of the black walls around her.

The footman opened the door and helped her out. "Thank you," she said. She left them and headed toward the theater. She should have a chaperone considering she was still technically unmarried. Most of the matrons had stopped paying her much mind. They all knew she was betrothed and would be a duchess one day. They didn't want to end up on the wrong side of Pearyn's patronage. One day she'd wield more power than them with that title. That is if she ever married the Duke of Partridgdon.

She entered the theater and headed toward the Earl of Harrington's theater box. Pearyn would have liked one of her own, but they wouldn't allow a woman to acquire one. She needed patronage for that, and she had none that she trusted with her money. Besides, her friends helped her and invited her to use their boxes often enough to satisfy her need to attend the theater.

When she reached the box it was empty. Pearyn frowned. Perhaps they were caught in the line of carriages and would be inside soon. In her normal seat a single hyacinth had been placed. It was a light blue violet, nearly the same shade as her gown, and probably a closer match to the shade of her eyes. A white ribbon was tied to it with a small card. Her name had been written on the front. She picked it up and turned the card over. The back simply said: *Journey's end in lover's meeting...* A line from the song Feste sings in the Twelfth Night.

"Pretty flowers," a man said from behind her. His tone was husky, like warm brandy and spice, and it was...familiar.

She turned and stared at the man. Pearyn didn't recognize him, but something was definitely familiar about him. He had emerald green eyes, golden blond hair, chiseled high cheekbones, and a full, very kissable mouth. She shook that thought away. Pearyn would not be kissing anyone. A memory flashed from the previous night...that didn't count. He'd kissed her and walked away. Pearyn narrowed her gaze. She couldn't tell by looking at him, because the library had been too dark, but she'd bet her entire inheritance that this man had been the same one that had kissed her. "Why are you here?" she asked. That sounded rather...stupid, but she couldn't seem to form more intelligent words.

He lifted a brow, almost mocking. No, there was no almost about it. He was mocking her. "It's the theater. What does one usually do at such a place?"

Pleasant kiss aside, all right it was more than pleasant, Pearyn decided she didn't like him, and she didn't know his name. She decided that derisive answers deserved calculating ones in turn. "Any number of things," she began. "Meeting friends, clandestine encounters with lovers, heckling actors on stage…" It was Pearyn's turn to lift a brow. "No one comes to see the performance. Which one are you hoping to achieve?" She didn't hold the contempt out of her tone. If he wanted to play games, he'd soon discover she was not the insipid young miss he may have considered her to be.

His lips twitched. He was struggling to hide his amusement and failing. Pearyn wanted to slap that glee off his face. Somehow she restrained herself from acting upon the urge. "And if I said I came to see you?"

She rolled her eyes. "You're lying." She stared down at the hyacinth she'd found on her chair. Could he be her admirer? No. That was ridiculous. "We've never met why would you wish to see me?" Where was the countesses?

He chuckled softly. "Sweet," the gentleman said. He held his hand on his chest, as if she'd injured him with her words. "You've forgotten about me so soon." He leaned down so his mouth was close to her ear. "And I thought we shared something special the night before."

She'd been nearly certain he was the man who'd

kissed her. He had just confirmed it. "Was that you?" She batted her eyelashes at him. "I suppose you are forgettable then."

He bared his teeth. "Pretty words," he said. "But a kiss like that is memorable."

Pearyn shrugged. "Perhaps for you it was." The curtains lifted. "It matters not. The play is about to start and I do not wish to miss a moment of it." She took her seat and nibbled on her bottom lip. The countesses were not there, and she feared all three had decided not to attend. She'd have to pay a few calls tomorrow to discover why they had stayed home. There had to be a good reason.

The man took a seat next to her. She really wished she had been introduced to him. Pearyn had a feeling she knew him somehow, but she couldn't place him. She was certain that they'd never encountered each other before that shared kiss. He was too beautiful to forget.

Pearyn lost herself in the play. At intermission the man leaned in and said, "How familiar are you with this play?"

She didn't wish to talk to him, but she did enjoy a good discussion. "I've read it several times, but this is the first I've seen it performed." That's why she'd recognized the quote left on the hyacinth.

The gentleman tilted his head to the side. "Do you believe love is worth this comedy of errors?"

Pearyn took a deep breath. "Love can be quite fulfilling, but it also can be quite painful…almost like a curse, as the play often suggests." She swallowed the lump that had formed in her throat. Pearyn wanted to believe in love. She'd witnessed it firsthand, but had never truly felt it. "Especially if it is unrequited."

"Do you love someone that does not return that emotion for you?" he asked softly.

She shook her head. "No. My situation is perhaps worse. I have a fiancé who doesn't love me, doesn't bother to acknowledge me, and probably wishes I don't exist. I'm in limbo, almost a hell of sorts, where I can't move forward and I'm fast losing any chance of a future." She turned toward him. "I can't love because I cannot afford a broken heart. That would be adding purgatory to mix with my hell. Never-ending grief would be my future, and that is no way to live."

The man grew quiet, and Pearyn wondered if her words had left a wound he couldn't shake. Was he trapped in a similar situation? Maybe she would ask him his name. If they shared a comparable misery perhaps they could be friends. She could use someone that could relate to her desolation.

The play resumed, and Pearyn forgot about the man beside her. So she didn't notice when he slipped out, and she missed her chance to acquire his name. Maybe the countesses could tell her. She'd ask all three of them when she paid a call on each of them.

CHAPTER 5

*P*earyn pulled her gloves on and headed toward the foyer. After the fiasco the theater had developed into after the unknown gentleman had joined her, she had to make those calls on her friends. They were up to something, but what she couldn't possibly decipher without more information.

"Beatrice," she called to her maid.

"Yes, my lady?" Beatrice asked from behind her, as they descended the stairs.

"I'm expecting the gowns I ordered from the seamstress today. When they arrive please unpack them so the wrinkles can be removed." She had plans for the new gowns. Usually she didn't bother, but she had sent around a message to her favorite seamstress and asked that she consider a few new designs for her. She had all of Pearyn's measurements and didn't need her for the fitting, and if something did turn out to be off, she'd pay a visit to make any changes. "I'll need to try them on to ensure they're a good fit." Her seamstress had worked much faster than she had anticipated, but she had a few gowns she'd already been working on for her. Lindy, her seamstress, must have realized it had been a while since she'd ordered anything new and anticipated the order, or she was hoping Pearyn would contact her. Either way, Pearyn intended on including a bonus for Lindy when she paid her for the gowns. "I'll return in a few hours after I have finished my calls. Have them readied."

"I will," Beatrice answered. They reached the front entrance. Beatrice reached for Pearyn's wrap and helped secure it in place. "All the gowns will be ready for you when you return." She curtsied and went back up the stairs. Beatrice was a good maid.

Pearyn walked out of her townhouse and headed down the street. Her friends didn't live far, and even in the colder weather, it was easier to walk than bother with a carriage. It didn't take her long to reach the first home, Lady Shelby's, and Charlotte's sister-in-law. Pearyn wasn't as close to her or the other countesses as she was to Charlotte, but they had welcomed her into their circle. She hoped she had not done something to offend any of them. Pearyn raised her hand and rapped on the door. The Shelby butler opened it and replied, "Lady Pearyn. The other ladies are already in the salon. Would you like me to take your wrap?" Pearyn frowned. Was she interrupting something? The butler seemed to think she was expected.

"Yes," she answered. He assisted her and hung her wrap on a nearby post. "I'll see myself to the salon if that is all right?"

"Of course," he said in a pleasant tone.

With those words she walked down the hallway to Kaitlin, Lady Shelby's private salon. Lady Shelby didn't visit with anyone other than her closest friends in her private salon. It didn't take long for her to reach the room. Once there she was pleasantly surprised to find not only Lady Harrington and Lady Asthey there but also Charlotte.

"Pear!" Her friend jumped up and rushed over to her side, then wrapped her arms around her in a hug. "I was going to stop and see you after my visit here, but this is a welcome surprise."

"I thought you were going to be away for a few more days." Charlotte stepped back and smiled. "Collin finished his assessment early. There are still so many repairs that need to be done to the house, but it is coming along nicely."

"Good," Pearyn replied almost absentmindedly. She had not expected to find Charlotte there. "Am I interrupting?" She glanced past Charlotte and met Lady Shelby's gaze.

"Not at all," Lady Shelby replied. Her smile was soft, almost shy, in response. She was the quietest one of the group and only spoke fervently when it was most important to her. "Please sit. Would you like tea?" She met Charlotte's gaze. "Can you pour her a cup?"

"No, thank you," she said with a shake of her head. "I'm fine without."

"Are you certain?" Charlotte asked. "It's no trouble."

"I am," she reassured her friend. "Sit with me."

"What brings you here?" Lady Harrington asked.

They definitely hadn't expected her by the puzzled expressions on their faces. "I was wondering what happened to everyone. The theater box was decidedly empty last night." Not entirely empty...but she wasn't ready to disclose that information yet. "I expected everyone here except Charlotte to be in attendance."

Lady Asthey sat forward. "We had no plans to attend the theater." She pushed her eyebrows together. "Why did you expect us?"

Pearyn frowned. "I received a note…" She hadn't considered that the note might not have been from her friends. "It indicated I should join the three of you there." Was someone having a good joke on her? Pearyn secretly fumed.

"I'm so sorry," Lady Harrington said. "I do not understand how that enormous of a mistake could have happened, but Samantha is right. We did not intend to go to the theater. Was it signed by one of us?"

Pearyn thought back to the note. "It hadn't been…" There was just a scribble across the card requesting she join them. "There was no seal on it either, now that I think about it. The note seemed so innocuous… It is a public place and we share a box. There was no reason for me to question it."

"That's rather frightening," Charlotte said in a somber tone. "I think you should stay away from anything unless you hear it directly from one of us. Was it overly distressing? Did anyone else join you?"

Only a strange golden haired gentleman... "No," she said. Pearyn didn't know why, but she didn't want to tell them about him. Then she'd let it all spill out, and she had no desire to tell them about the gifts or that kiss... "It was just a bit lonely." That was not entirely a lie. She'd been feeling that more than she'd like of late. "I'm glad that you didn't abandon me on purpose though."

"We would never do that," Lady Shelby said ardently. "You are our friend."

No they wouldn't... So had her mystery gentleman arranged for their private time in the box? Anyone could have seen them there together. What did the gossipmongers of society think of that? Should she care? "I am grateful either way." She stood. "I'd like to stay but I am going to the bookstore. I'm lacking anything stimulating to read." She had a desperate need to leave and analyze everything in private.

"I'll go with you," Charlotte said, and set her teacup down. "We can have a nice chat on our walk there."

Pearyn repressed a groan. She'd have to go to the bookstore now that Charlotte had invited herself along. She would have gone straight home and pretended to have gone otherwise. "What a lovely idea."

They both left the salon and went to the foyer. They grabbed their wraps and donned them, then left the Shelby townhouse. The bookstore was a bit longer of a walk than Pearyn would have liked in the cold weather, but she didn't let herself think about that. "You have news?"

"I do," Charlotte said. "I finished my book."

"Oh," Pearyn exclaimed. "That's wonderful. I cannot wait to read it."

"Collin is going to help me submit it to publishers. With him as my agent there is hope that it'll be accepted, but we shall see."

"It will be," Pearyn told her. "You're a brilliant novelist." Charlotte's dream had always been to write a book. She'd gone to great lengths to be able to pursue that dream. Her aspirations had changed a little bit after meeting and falling in love with Collin, but it had only expanded into a bigger dream. One that it appeared Charlotte would be achieving soon.

Most of the walk to the bookstore was in silence. When they arrived at their favorite bookseller, they went inside. The warm air hit Pearyn, and she sighed. She was not made for cold weather. She turned to Charlotte. "I'm going to the back to see what new books there might be on Greek mythology." It was one of her latest obsessions.

Charlotte wrinkled her nose. "I'm going to look at the novels. I don't want to study anything factual. I want to be swept away on an adventure."

"There's adventure in fiction, true, but there is also travel in the truth. It opens the mind to places and things that you can only imagine."

"Go find your books," Charlotte replied. "I'll stick to mine."

They separated and Pearyn went to the section she wanted to explore. She stopped short when the golden-haired gentleman was there. He had the very book she hoped to obtain in his hands. It was doubtful the bookseller had more than one. She stomped forward and stopped when she reached him. "What are you doing here?"

He lifted his head and met her gaze. He glanced toward her, then at the shelves. "Is this not a bookstore?"

Oh… "Yes, of course it is," she fumed. "But what are you doing inside it?"

He closed the book he'd been skimming and said, "What does one usually do inside a bookstore?" He lifted a mocking brow. "Do you suppose I am doing something nefarious?"

She wasn't sure what he might or might not do. Pearyn had a feeling he was the reason she'd attended the theater. She couldn't prove it though. "Can I have that book?" She tapped the book he had in his hands.

"No," he answered. "It's a gift for my fiancée. She's been hoping for it and I want to surprise her with it."

Her mouth fell open in shock. He'd kissed her! The rogue had not even married his intended bride, and he was already looking for his pleasures elsewhere. She lifted her chin the disdain dripped from her tone as she spoke, "You sir are the worst sort of gentleman." With those words, she turned on her heels and stormed away. His chuckles followed behind her in her wake, and she could have sworn he said, "But you love me anyway…"

She did not. He was a scoundrel. It didn't matter if she found him attractive. He was betrothed, and it hurt more than she wanted to admit that he was unavailable. She had enjoyed his company, and that kiss. Part of her had hoped he was her secret admirer. But he couldn't be if he was already attached to another woman, and if he was the one sending her gifts, well then, he was much worse than she'd believed. She didn't need a man like that in her life.

CAMERON FROWNED. HIS PLANS WITH PEARYN HAD been going so well. He feared he might have overplayed his hands with her. She was so lovely when she was angry, but she was beautiful either way. Maybe his parents had done him a favor by selling his hand in marriage. He'd never openly admit that...to anyone.

He may have made a mistake.

Hell, he'd probably made several. Perhaps this was always meant to be their path, though. If he'd stayed and they had married years before they wouldn't be the people they'd turned into. They may never have discovered who they were meant to be. He would have resented her even more than he had over the years. Now though, if he played it right, they had a real chance at something much more special.

She didn't realize it, but he was courting her. This was a way for them to discover things about themselves that they wouldn't have otherwise. If the duke showed up at her door, she'd close herself off to him. He was no fool. She resented him as much as he had her.

All secrets would be revealed later. Hopefully she didn't hate him when they were…

THE GROUND HAD BEEN COVERED IN WHITE FOR DAYS now, but it was the first day in as long as Pearyn could recall that didn't make her want to crawl back under the covers and hibernate until spring.

"Charlotte," she said. "What made you think I'd enjoy riding in Hyde Park?" In her opinion, willingly doing any form of exercise outdoors in winter was insane. "Do you not have better things to occupy your time? Did you not purchase a new book the other day?"

Pearyn didn't want to think too hard about her time in the bookstore, and her encounter with the golden-haired gentleman. She had been disappointed two-fold. He was attached to another lady, and he had refused to let her have the one book she'd hoped to find in the store.

"Because you are too much of a recluse of late. Someone had to drag you outside…even if it is kicking and screaming." Charlotte grinned.

Pearyn stuck her tongue out. The last time they'd been in Hyde Park, Charlotte had been riding in breeches. It had been a bit of a scandal that she had created on purpose. Her friend could be brave, much, much braver, than Pearyn. She pretended at times that she was, but where it mattered, she cowered. Somehow she had to find a way to move forward. She didn't know how to reach the Duke of Partridgdon, but it was time to end her betrothal. She didn't need him, or his title. At the start of the new year she'd visit his solicitors and have them forward a letter to him, maybe sooner if she found time. She'd pen the missive when she returned home. If she was destined to be a spinster, so be it. It was better to accept it, then hold on to something that never was truly hers to begin with.

She hadn't received any more special gifts either. Perhaps the golden-haired gentleman had been her secret admirer, and after his admission, had decided against sending any further enticements. It was sad, and difficult to swallow, in a way. Maybe he would have sent her that book she'd wanted, but she'd caught him with it and he had decided against it. She doubted that, but she had really wanted it, and it would have been nice if he intended it for her.

"I'll race you." Pearyn had an idea that might

appeal to her friend. Charlotte never could resist a dare. The park was nearly empty, but there were still inhabitants. During the warmer months, the park was full. A nice race between her and Charlotte was doable now.

Charlotte flicked the reins. "You're going to lose." She was off before Pearyn had a chance to react.

She might come to regret this race, but the pure joy on Charlotte's face was worth any risk. Pearyn loved her friend so much. She was the only person she had truly cared about through the years. At least she had her, even if she had to share her with Collin, and one day their children. That would have to be enough.

Pearyn flicked the reins. Her horse took off after Charlotte. She'd never catch up to her, but she had to at least try. It wouldn't be much of a win if she didn't put the effort in. Her horse shot off into a gallop. Pearyn slipped in her saddle and she screamed. Somehow she had to slow the horse because she was about to fall off her horse. Her sudden inspiration to race against Charlotte didn't seem so bright right now. She was heading straight for a bunch of trees. Charlotte had veered left, but Pearyn was not going to be able to avoid them.

She cursed under her breath and tried to pull on

her reins. It ended up being more of a gentle tug than the hard yank she'd been going for. Still, her horse slowed a little, but not enough, not nearly enough... As she neared the trees, a gentleman stepped from behind them. A flash of golden hair caught her attention, but it was more a passing thought. It couldn't be the same gentleman—fate wouldn't do that to her...

As she neared him she lost all ability to remain in the saddle, and slipped off of it, and landed right on top of him. He wrapped his arms around her and they rolled across the ground once they made impact. Pearyn's arm hurt and she was having difficulty regaining her bearing. "My apologies," she said. "I should never had agreed to that race."

"It's quite all right," he said. "It made for an interesting change of scenery...and I cannot complain. I would not have found you in my arms otherwise."

Pearyn groaned. It was him. Why did he seem to be everywhere lately? "It had to be you." She glanced up, and he flashed her a sinful half smile. It sent shivers down her spine and she had to resist the urge to lean closer and press her lips to his. That kiss they shared lingered in the forefront of her mind, and nothing seemed to make her forget it had happened.

"I like you too," he said. "But you didn't have to fall at my feet. I'm happy to give you my attention. There's no need for dramatics."

She shoved her hands into his chest and said, "Release me."

"Are you certain?" His tone was husky. "I think you want to be in my arms."

"Ohhh…." She pushed him again. "I've had enough of you."

"Sweet," he began. "I do believe you're lying to yourself. You want more than you're letting yourself admit." He winked. Why did he have to be so gorgeous and charming?

"You keep telling yourself that." She glared at him. "Now please, let me up."

He rolled them to their sides, and then he released her. The gentleman stood and held his hand out to her. "Let me assist you."

"No, thank you," she ground out. Pearyn stood and brushed the snow off her skirts, then stalked away. She grabbed the reins of her horse that had thankfully stopped nearby. At least one thing was going right…

Pearyn did not look back at the gentleman. She wanted to. She was drawn to him, and her feelings for him confused her. Pearyn hated that her heart skipped a beat when he was near, and she wanted to be with him. He made her feel good and she feared that the emotions growing inside her would lead to a broken heart. He was not available to her, and she had to remind her heart of that fact as often as possible.

CHAPTER 6

Christmas Eve

*P*earyn had chosen one of her new gowns for the ball Charlotte had decided to host to celebrate the beginning of Christmastide. The twelve days of Christmas was a magical time of the year. It was perhaps the only time she didn't mind the cold, or snow, or well, anything about winter. She had already sent the gifts she'd purchased for her friends to their residences. In a perfect world she would be with them while they opened them, but she was happy that they would have them to enjoy later. The joy, for her, was in giving them, and in a time when she had experienced more melancholy than she'd like, it gave her some moment of happiness.

Beatrice strolled into Pearyn's bedchamber. "Are you ready to put on your gown, my lady?"

"Yes," Pearyn said. Beatrice had already styled her hair. Her midnight tresses were mostly pulled back away from her face. The side portions were tied behind her head with green and white ribbons, but the rest had been left loose down her back in soft waves.

"Very well," Beatrice said and went to retrieve her gown. Her undergarments were already in place. The dress was a vibrant green lace over a lighter, almost golden, green silk. It had full skirts that shimmied a little when she moved. The bodice hugged her breasts and was overlayed with silk that wrapped around her upper arms. It was truly a gorgeous gown.

"Here we are," Beatrice said as she carried it over to Pearyn. "Step into it my lady and I'll pull it up around your chemise, and straighten it all out. We don't want to ruin your hair."

It took the two of them to get the gown in place, but it had been worth it. She might never be a duchess, but she certainly felt like one in this dress. Beatrice finished fastening the back of the gown and then tied it closed. "There, my lady," she said with a pleased tone. "You're prettier than a princess. Have you decided on what necklace you would like to wear?"

She reached up and touched her neck. Pearyn didn't have a lot of jewelry, but she did have her mother's necklace. She rarely wore it. Pearyn considered it as more of a special occasion necklace and could count on one hand how many times she'd allowed it to grace her neck. It was a pendant of pearls and diamonds that almost resembled wings the way it flared out. It had a gold chain attached to each end that allowed it to be fastened in the middle. Pearyn turned toward Beatrice. "Yes, will you retrieve my mother's necklace?" It might not be a special occasion, but Pearyn felt extraordinary, and it seemed right.

Beatrice went to the jewelry box and brought the necklace back. She draped it around Pearyn's neck and fastened the clasp. Pearyn touched the necklace, and for the first time, she wasn't sad at the thought of her mother. Maybe she was finally able to let go of that pain. Her mother wasn't a bad person. Pearyn didn't agree with a lot of the choices she'd made, but her heart had been in the right place. She had wanted what was best for her daughter, and she had believed becoming a duchess was going to make Pearyn's life better. If her betrothed had wanted to marry her, perhaps that would have been a good thing. Considering he had disappeared at the first opportunity had made it clear to Pearyn he didn't want her. Instead of letting that control her life, she'd made the decision to make the best of a horrible situation. No one knew how much pain she'd been in over the years. It was past time to let it all go. She'd written that letter and had it delivered to the Duke of Partridgdon's solicitors. Wherever the duke had disappeared to, he'd know soon enough he was free to do as he pleased. Not that it had ever stopped him before. He would just know, soon, that he was free from his marriage contract. If he had found someone else to give his heart to, he could openly do so.

"Thank you," she said to Beatrice. "You can have the rest of the evening off. I'm going to the foyer. My wrap is already downstairs and I should be able to put it on myself." The truth was, she wanted a few moments alone before she left for the ball. When she arrived Charlotte would demand a lot of her time. At least when she wasn't solely focusing her attention on Collin.

"Have a pleasant evening," Beatrice said. "And Happy Christmas."

Pearyn smiled. "Enjoy your holiday." She'd given the entire staff off for the next couple days. Cook had made some bread, and simple meals for her to serve herself while they were gone. She didn't need much, anyway.

Beatrice left Pearyn alone, and she let her smile fade from her face. She didn't have to put up any more pretenses now that she was alone. Pearyn strolled to her window and looked outside. Stars blanketed the night sky, but there was no snow falling. The walk to Charlotte's home should be uneventful. There would still be a lot of people attending, and carriages would litter the streets as guests arrived, but at least she wouldn't be stuck in that crush. She was grateful her friend still remained close, at least while she was in London.

With a sigh, she stepped away from the window and left her chambers. She walked down the stairs and lifted her wrap off a nearby hook. It was a white velvet with a fur lining that enveloped her in warmth. Her butler had already retired for the evening, so she let herself out.

It didn't take her long to reach the Frossly townhouse. Charlotte's husband, Collin, the Earl of

Frossly, was working diligently to restore his ancestral home, but his townhouse was already in exquisite condition. The steps leading to the entrance had dark green boughs along the side tied with red ribbons to hold them in place. She'd been right about the line of carriages that would be waiting to reach the Frossly townhouse. The ball was in full swing, and there were plenty of individuals arriving fashionably late, including herself.

Pearyn strolled to the entrance and knocked. The butler opened and greeted her. "Good evening, Lady Pearyn," he said. "Please come in." He took her wrap and handed it to a footman. "Do you require an escort?" he asked.

"I can find my own way," Pearyn said.

"Very well, my lady," he said, and smiled. "They'll announce you when you enter the ball."

This was Charlotte's first major social event since her marriage. She'd been so focused on finishing her novel she hadn't bothered. As a result, she had gone a little overboard. Luckily, there were still several members of the ton in town for the holiday season, and had decided that her ball was the place to be.

After she was announced Pearyn went to find Charlotte. She skimmed the sides of the dance floor until she was on the far, middle side of the room. When they announced the next guest, she froze in her steps.

"His grace, the Duke of Partridgdon," the footman said loudly for the entire ballroom to hear.

Slowly, Pearyn turned and met his gaze. He had golden blond hair that shimmered in the light, and he was dressed in all black, except for the starch white of his shirt and cravat. She couldn't see his eyes, but she knew they were emerald green. Pearyn knew this, because he was the same man she'd been encountering across London for days. The very gentleman that she'd been attracted to, had started to fall for, and who she had believed to be unavailable, was her fiancé.

Instead of facing him, she exited by the closest side door and rushed out of the room. This was too much, and she couldn't breathe. He was here, and if she wanted him, she could have him. The one man she'd desired was…hers, and she'd set him free…

CAMERON HAD SIGHTED HER THE INSTANT HE'D stepped into the ballroom. She was as lovely as he remembered, perhaps even more beautiful if that was possible. It was time to claim her, and he couldn't wait to kiss her again. He hoped she'd forgive his subterfuge, but he had to know her, and ensure that he could love her. He had no doubts. Pearyn was special and he couldn't lose her.

His solicitors had sent him her letter. When he read her words his heart had nearly dropped out of his chest. She didn't want him. He might be too late, but he had to try. Never once, in his planning, had he thought she'd break their betrothal. He'd overestimated her willingness to wait for him. She'd been patient for so long, and apparently, she'd lost all hope he'd ever follow through and marry her. He had to convince her to give him another chance.

She had fled the ballroom, and he had to discern where she could have gone. He rushed across the room and went through the doors she'd exited from. They led to a balcony that led to the garden. Cold air blew over him and he shivered. She didn't like the cold. It was one of the first things he'd discovered about her. His Pearyn must really need to escape him if she'd gone willingly into the frigid night.

"Pearyn," he called. There was no answer from her. He moved down the stairs and into the garden. It was a barren landscape frozen over with ice and snow. As he approached a fountain depicting a couple in love, he discovered her staring at them. "Sweet," he said. "Why don't you come back inside."

She turned toward him. "And why should I?"

There was sadness in her eyes he wished he could erase. "Because it is a tiny bit cold out here. We can go inside, where its warm, and discuss this." He hoped he could convince her to go back into the house. They could find a quiet place inside to talk, and he could make his confessions there.

She shrugged. "I don't feel anything."

Cameron stepped closer to her. "I don't believe that." He wasn't sure if she meant the cold, or emotions. Either way, his reply still fit. "You feel too much, and there is nothing wrong with that." He took another step. "We do need to talk."

"About?" She lifted a brow. "I don't think I owe you anything. You might need to explain a few things, but I'm not sure I care. I set you free." She met his gaze boldly. "I assume you received my letter considering you're in London and have been for what appears to be some time. You knew how to find me and have been ensuring we would cross paths several times over the past few weeks. Why bother? What did you hope to gain?" Her voice shook a little as she spoke. "Did you enjoy making a fool out of me?"

"Of course not," he said, his voice hoarse with emotion. He lifted his hand and cupped her cheek. "That was never my purpose."

When he set out to court her, he'd decided that she would be more herself if she didn't know who he was, but he'd overplayed his hand. She doubted him, and his intentions. He was losing her, and he might not be able to make it right.

"Then what did you hope to achieve?" Her voice softened a little and she placed her hand over his. "Why are you doing any of this?"

"Because I had to know," he told her. "This was the only way..."

"For what?" She stepped away from him. Anger was infused in her voice as she spoke. "None of this makes any sense."

He closed his eyes and took a dep breath He was handing all of this wrong. Cameron reached inside his pocket and pulled out a box. He brushed his thumb across the top and considered his next words. "Our betrothal was decided by our parents. It was cold, calculating, and formal. My father gave me no choice, and yes, at the first opportunity I ran. I didn't know who I was. How could I possibly make anyone a good husband?"

She lifted a brow. "And did you discover yourself on your travels?"

He moved closer. "I did," he said. "When I returned this time…"

"Wait," she interrupted. "This time? You have been back in London before now?"

"Several times," he admitted. "But I wasn't here long when I did, and I wasn't ready to face you before now." Cameron sighed. "I'm sorry for that. I should have had some contact with you, but I'd be lying if I said I didn't resent you, resent the decision that had been made for me."

"You think it was any easier for me." She shivered, but her eyes blazed with fury. "I'm the one that had to face everyone and pretend I was all right with your abandonment. I had to move forward and make the best out of a terrible situation. I wasn't the coward."

"You're right," he said. "I was weak, but I was also young, and quite foolish." He wanted to pull her into his arms, but he refrained. She wasn't ready for any affection yet. "It's why I knew I had to earn your trust. To woo you and hopefully, if I'm lucky enough, win the right to be in your life." He stepped a little closer, hoping to entice her into his arms with his proximity. "I sent you gifts, I tried my hand at poetry," he confesses. "It's the twenty-fourth…"

"So you think it's that easy," she said a little sarcastically. "You make a few confessions and all my doubts will be washed away?"

"Yes," he said in earnest. "Well, not exactly. I'm sure there is a lot we will have to discuss." He brushed a stray lock away. "I don't accept your decision to end our betrothal. I want to marry you." He met her gaze. "Not because my parent, or yours willed it, but because I love you, and I cannot imagine a life without you in it." He opened the box and revealed the pear-shaped diamond with amethyst's surrounding it to her. "Please marry me."

A tear fell down her eyes. "You're my secret admirer."

"I am," he admitted. "And I promise, if you'll be my duchess I'll spend the rest of my life ensuring you never doubt me again. Please," he said. "Say yes…"

She stared at the ring. "All right," she said. "On one condition."

"Anything," he agreed. He'd give her whatever she desired as long as she married him. Cameron had made a lot of mistakes and he hoped in time, he could rectify them.

"I don't want to wait long for a wedding." She smiled. "I had this long engagement, and well, it didn't end the way I had hoped. This time, I want to marry as soon as possible."

His lips twitched as he fought a smile. "I do have connections and if you desire it…I could arrange for a special license." What he didn't say was he had already secured one, hoping she'd want to marry as soon as possible. Cameron was done waiting and wanted to start the new year with her as his wife.

"Perfect," she said and stepped closer. "What are you waiting for?" She lifted a brow. "Kiss me."

"I thought you'd never ask." He had stopped feeling the cold a while ago, but he should still take her inside soon. But not before he kissed her at least once. He pressed his lips to hers, and it was as magical as he remembered.

EPILOGUE

The next day...

It was Christmas, and his wedding day. His bride wore a gown of shimmering silver, and her hair had been left completely down. The dark waves had flowed enticingly down her back. They were at his townhouse. She had given her servants the holiday off, and luckily, he had kept a few in residence. He had a vicar ready to perform the ceremony earlier that morning. Pearyn was now his wife, and he had a few more gifts for her.

He pulled her into his arms, "Merry Christmas, love."

"Merry Christmas," she said. "What are we going to do with our day?"

"I plan on making love to my wife," he said. "But first..." He pressed his lips to hers and kissed her until she was breathless. "I have something for you."

Cameron left her alone in the sitting room. He went to his study and retrieved the package he had intended to deliver to her days ago...that is, until she'd discovered him with it in his hands. He couldn't have given it to her then. She would have realized who he was much sooner than he wanted her to if he had. With the package in his hands, he returned to the sitting room and presented it to her. "This is for you."

She tore the paper off and gasped. "The book I wanted." The gleeful grin on her face made his heart burst with pleasure. Pearyn hugged it to her chest. "I was so mad you wouldn't let me buy it."

"I couldn't," he said. "I was already going to purchase it for you, as one of your gifts."

She chuckled lightly. "I ruined some of your plans didn't I?"

"Sweet," he began. "You were one surprise after the next. Not every encounter was planned, and that day in the bookstore was one of them."

"The theater?"

He grimaced. "I should apologize for that. I lured you out with the promise of an evening with your friends. I hope you were not too disappointed."

"I was at first," she admitted. "But I'm glad you were there. It was when I started to fall in love. You engaged my mind, and I found you intriguing, despite the kiss in the darkened library. I wanted to know more about you—even when I found you irritating."

"I suspected as much," he confessed. "But I started to worry that night I had caused you too much pain, and my deception would ruin us before we had a real chance at a beginning. I'm glad I was wrong." He took the book from her arms and set it on the table. "Thank you for forgiving me. I know I'm difficult at times, but I do intend to do my best to be a wonderful husband to you. Even if it takes me the rest of my life."

"That's how it usually works." She laughed. "Don't worry. I don't expect you to be perfect. I just want you, to be you. It's why I love you after all."

"Do me one favor," he said as he pulled her into his arms. "Promise me you'll refrain from horse racing with your friend. I lost several years off my life when you fell off that horse."

"I will try," she said. "I cannot make any promises. Charlotte can be quite...convincing."

Cameron kissed her cheek. "I suppose that will have to do." He adored her. When he returned to London, he didn't think he could ever be this happy. He was glad he was wrong. Pearyn was always meant to be his, and he intended to treasure the gift he'd been given. It was the best present he could have ever been given, and it was a Christmas he would not forget. He pressed his lips to hers and became lost in the magic of her.

AFTERWORD

Thank you so much for taking the time to read my book.

Your opinion matters!

Please take a moment to review this book on your favorite review site and share your opinion with fellow readers.

www.authordawnbrower.com

LADY PEAR'S SONNET

Cold is the frigid winds of winter
Frozen is the ties that bind
My purpose will never splinter
For it's your love I seek, and will find

Distance has not been kind
For it has kept us apart
You're not far from my mind
And I hope to win your heart

With this gift my intentions are clear
Soon we will meet once more
And I'll hold you, my dear
On the night marked twenty-four

All doubts will be washed away
And love will reign on that day...

ABOUT THE AUTHOR

USA TODAY Bestselling author, DAWN BROWER writes both historical and contemporary romance. There are always stories inside her head; she just never thought she could make them come to life. That creativity has finally found an outlet.

Growing up she was the only girl out of six children. She raised two boys into productive young men. There is never a dull moment in her life. Reading books is her favorite hobby and she loves all genres.

She is active on Facebook, Twitter, and Instagram. To follow her or can find more about her check out her website for the pertinent information:

www.authordawnbrower.com

ALSO BY DAWN BROWER

Never Disregard a Wallflower

Never Dare a Hellion

Never Deceive a Bluestocking

Never Disrespect a Governess

Never Desire a Duke

Lady Be Wicked/Wayward Dukes'/Wicked Widows'

Her Rogue for One Night (Wicked Widows)

A Lady Never Tells

Her Duke to Beguile

Her Duke of Sin (Wayward Dukes')

Her Duke to Savor (Wayward Dukes')

Coming in 2024/2025

A Lady Never Confesses

A Lady Never Forgets

Her Rogue for Christmas (Wicked Widows)

Her Rogue to Kiss Good Morning (Wicked Widows)

Her Duke to Seduce (Wayward Dukes')

Her Duke to Tempt (Wayward Dukes')

CONTEMPORARY

Stand alone:

Deadly Benevolence

Snowflake Kisses

Kindred Lies

Sparkle City

Diamonds Don't Cry

Hooking a Firefly

Novak Springs

Cowgirl Fever

Dirty Proof

Unbridled Pursuit

Sensual Games

Christmas Temptation

Daring Love

Passion and Lies

Desire and Jealousy

Seduction and Betrayal

Begin Again

There You'll Be

Better as a Memory

Won't Let Go

Heart's Intent

One Heart to Give

Unveiled Hearts

Heart of the Moment

Thank you so much for taking the time to read my book.

Your opinion matters!

Please take a moment to review this book on your favorite review site and share your opinion with fellow readers.

www.authordawnbrower.com

ACKNOWLEDGMENTS

Special thanks to Victoria Miller always supporting me. I couldn't do this without out your awesomeness, and being one of my best friends.

Elizabeth Evans, you are equally important. Thank you for reading all my roughest work and helping me improve it, and more importantly, thank you for being you, my friend, and for being a part of my life.

EXCERPT: THE VIXEN IN RED

BLUESTOCKINGS DEFYING ROGUES BOOK
EIGHT

DAWN BROWER

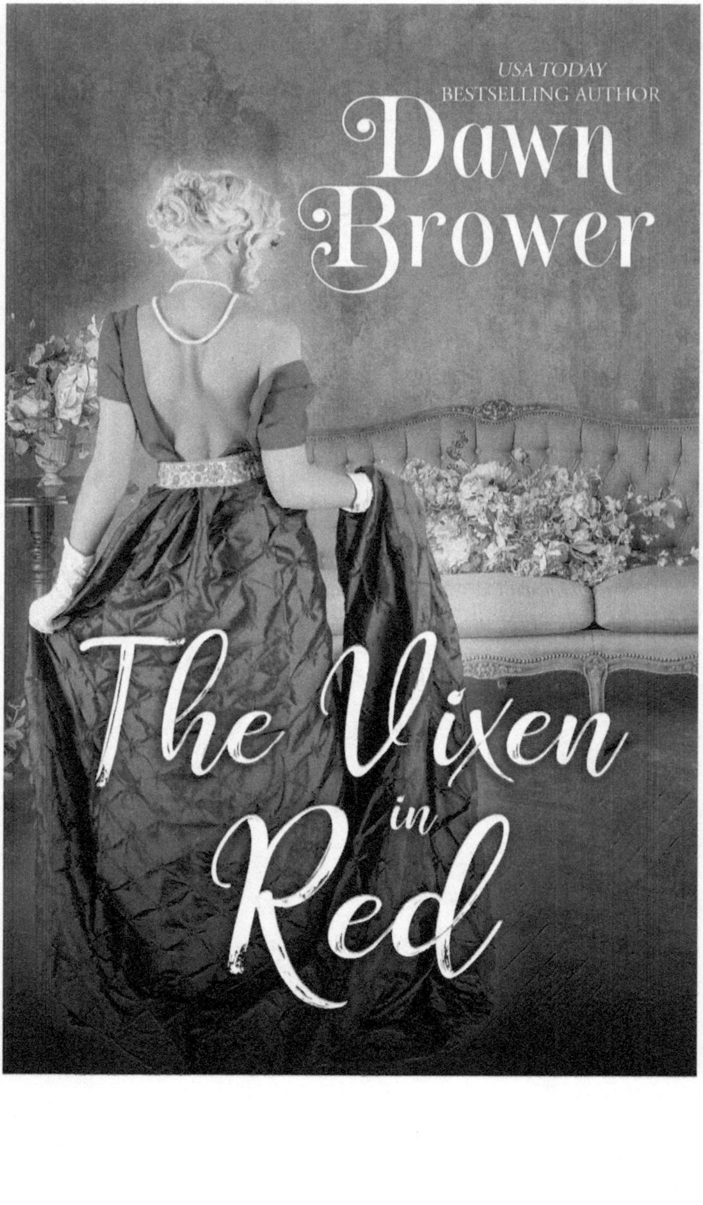
USA TODAY
BESTSELLING AUTHOR
Dawn
Brower
The Vixen
in
Red

CHAPTER 1

The sun was high in the sky and the wind blew lightly across Lady Charlotte Rossington's face. The garden at her father's, the Marquess of Seabrook's, London house had started to bloom. The flowers were mere buds, but they showed promise of being true beauties when they reached their peak. She reached down and brushed her fingers over the tiny buds and smiled.

"Are you certain this plan of yours is wise?" Her closest friend, Lady Pearyn Treedale asked. Her dark locks were pinned back into an intricate chignon, but a few tendrils had escaped in the breeze. Her blue eyes were the same shade as the sky. She was a true beauty and one day would be a duchess, if her fiancé ever deigned to return to England. Pear didn't mind his absence. She'd enjoyed being out in society without having to bother with finding a suitor. In some ways Charlotte envied her. She very much did not want to partake in any society events.

"It's the only way I can make my mother understand my wishes. Her only desire is to see me married and having babies." Charlotte wrinkled her nose in distaste. "I have more wants and desires than can be found in wedding vows and a lifetime of marriage. She may have found happiness with my father, but I would prefer to have much more than love to sustain me in my future." Maybe one day she wouldn't mind finding a man to give her heart to, but not for a long time. Charlotte wanted time to be alone, explore *who* she was deep inside, and write. She had so many ideas, and she wanted to have time to put the stories inside her head down. Sharing those stories with the world was her greatest dream. She would not be able to do any of that if her mother forced her to participate in the season.

Pear took a deep breath. "I understand, I do, but I cannot help wishing there was a better way." She twisted her mouth into a frown. It was not a pretty look on such a lovely face. "The scandal…"

"Is the reason I'm doing it at all," she reminded her friend. "My mother won't have any choice. She'll have to let me return to Seabrook. There I can weather the scandal and I'll be left in peace to write my first novel. It will work, I know it will." Her mother, Rosanna, the Marchioness of Seabrook, would be livid.

"I still do not like it. With you at Seabrook I'll be left alone in London all season. I'll miss you." Pear sighed. "And with you in seclusion your mother will not have a house party as she usually does. The one at Weston Manor will also be off limits for you. This seems extreme. Is writing your book worth being without any social interactions for months?"

She nodded her head vigorously. "Yes, yes, and yes," Charlotte said. The very thought of being alone to write…it filled her heart with happiness. "It won't be so terrible. We can still write each other and I'll have my family. Well, mother and father. I'm not certain what Rhys will decide to do. He might spend time in London with his wife."

Before her brother Rhys, the Earl of Carrick had married Lady Hyacinth, Charlotte had been thrilled at the idea of attending balls, soirées, musicals, anything that involved society. Her young heart had seen it as an opportunity, and in some ways it had been. The first year had been wondrous. Until she thought she'd fallen in love, and the rogue broke her heart. She gave up on finding someone. It hurt too much when the gentleman of her dreams crushed her fragile heart. She'd much rather take control of her life, and this scandal was the first step.

Pear tapped her fingers on the bench she sat on as Charlotte paced the garden path near it. "I suppose you wish for me to accompany you on this endeavor of yours."

"I would like it if you would," she said. "It gives my statement credence." The ton would notice Charlotte either way, but with Pear they would also gain the attention of any gentleman that happened to be nearby. Considering her affianced state it drew them all to her side. They thought they might coax her in breaking her engagement. What they didn't understand was that she liked being engaged; however, Pear had no desire to actually be married. She didn't want love any more than Charlotte did.

"Very well," she agreed. "I'll be glad to assist you in ruining yourself." She sighed heavily. "It is all quite dramatic. I hope that the end result is as you hope. I would hate for this elaborate scheme to be for naught."

"So you have mentioned several times." Charlotte grinned. "You truly are the greatest friend a lady could have." Then she clapped her hands with excitement. "I cannot wait."

"I can," Pear said dryly. "Once this is done I'll not likely see you until Christmastide."

"Don't be sour," Charlotte chastised her. "It is unbecoming."

"Now you *sound* like your mother," Pear said distastefully. "I don't think you're as unalike as you claim."

They might have some similarities, but there were not many. "We don't even look much alike. My coloring is more like my father's." Her hair had the same golden hue as her father's but her eyes were a blue shade somewhere in-between her mother and father's. Even her brother favored their father in looks. It was odd that neither one of them looked much like their mother. "Mother has complained about that often enough. She once said that if she hadn't given birth to us she wouldn't have believed us to be her children. It was very crass of her to say aloud." She giggled. "Though to be fair we were being minxes at the time."

"I do not doubt that," Pear told her. "You can be quite the hellion from time to time." She narrowed her gaze. "After this they'll consider you more of a vixen. Are you prepared for all the negative gossip?"

She had thought long and hard about it. Charlotte wouldn't enjoy what some in society would openly say about her. Some of it might even... sting. "It won't be anything resembling enjoyment, but I do believe I can withstand even the harshest of criticisms." Most of which would come from her own mother's sharp tongue. "Once I'm back at Seabrook I won't be privy to it any longer. So I can pretend they aren't saying anything at all. I'll be peacefully writing and forgetting the scandal. I will be all right." She smiled at Pear. "I do appreciate your concern for my welfare."

"Since you are resigned," Pear began. "Then we should prepare for this scandal of yours. I'll have the stables prepare our horses. Meet me there after you've made your wardrobe adjustments."

"Perfect," Charlotte said. "I'll meet you in the stable in twenty minutes. It should not take me long. We need to be away from the house and in Hyde Park before my parent's return from their luncheon with the Duke and Duchess of Weston."

"Shoo," Pear replied and waved her hands at her. "There isn't a moment to lose."

Charlotte sprinted to the house and ran up to her bedchamber. Once there she stripped her gown, chemise, and shift off. Then she proceeded to change into a pair of her brother's old breeches, linen shirt, waistcoat, and jacket. She had been lucky enough to locate an old pair of his riding boots as well. Charlotte let her hair down from the chignon and plaited it, then twisted it in a knot at her nape. Once her hair was secured she slid a gentleman's hat on top her head. If not for her bosom and curves she might have been mistaken for a man at first glance. Satisfied with her handiwork she rushed down the stairs; careful to ensure no one noticed her, then went out to the stable.

Pear was already seated on her horse, and a groomsman held the reins to Charlotte's mare. She didn't ask him for assistance mounting. Charlotte strode to the block and slid on to the horse herself. Breeches were so freeing! She would have to figure out ways to wear them more often. She could ride like a man and not worry over a sidesaddle. Charlotte had instructed Pear to request a regular saddle. She was glad to see the groom had followed her directions. She turned to Pear and asked, "Are you ready?"

"Are we taking a chaperone?"

"That would defeat the purpose don't you think?" She nibbled on her bottom lip. "Are you worried about your reputation?" Charlotte didn't want to cause her friend any harm.

"I will be all right either way," Pear told her. "I don't have to worry about securing a good match. I'm flush with funds and I even have a fiancé if he decides traveling the continent is boring and returns to England. I was uncertain how much of a scandal you wished to cause is all."

"Well if you don't mind…"

"I do not," Pear reassured Charlotte, then pressed a knee into the side of her horse and guided the mare into a walk. Charlotte did the same, and then they started on their path to Hyde Park.

They did not converse for most of the trek to the park. Charlotte was too nervous to find words. So far everything had gone as planned. The rest had to follow suit. Otherwise the entire scheme would have been for nothing. She pressed her lips into a line as she anxiously rode beside Pear. Finally, they reached the park and steered the horses to the correct path. Hyde Park was the place to be seen and a large portion of the ton showed up to walk or ride in the late afternoon. There were perhaps not as many in the park as usual, but that was in large because it was not yet the full season. Early in spring was still early for the Season, as the gentry would not start to fully return to town until May. Still, there was enough of the upper crust in Hyde Park for Charlotte's purpose.

"Are they all looking at us?" she said in a loud whisper to Pear.

"Oh, yes," she reassured her. "There are quite a few discussions, and a few pointed glances, and fingers in your direction.

She hated being the center of attention. Charlotte had never wanted to be the belle of the ball. It would be much more to her liking if she could dance a couple of times, then retreat to the library. Occasionally a ball could be fun, but more often than not she'd hated them. "Good." The influx of gossipmongers would ensure that she would be at Seabrook by the end of the week...maybe sooner.

"You were right," Pear said. "Wearing men's clothing certainly caught their attention. Probably more than you anticipated." There was a bit of awe in her voice as she glanced around the park. "You still want to do one full round around the loop?"

"Yes," she said. "It has to be complete."

Though she was starting to wonder if she had lost her mind. The more they moved through the park the more the members of the ton started to talk...and loudly. She heard several unkind words she had wished she hadn't. Charlotte reminded herself that this had been what she wanted. It didn't hurt any less…

They reached the end of the path and the exit to the park was finally in sight. She froze. Her parents were strolling into the park with the Duke and Duchess of Weston. Charlotte had not anticipated that outcome. She thought she'd have time to go home and change. Then let the gossip come to them. Her mother's eyes widened, and her father turned toward her. His eyes glittered with disappointment. That hurt more than the harsh words. She hated displeasing her father…

Charlotte swallowed hard and held her head high. The time for turning back had passed the moment she left the townhouse in men's breeches. She had done this on purpose and now she had to pay the price for it…whatever that may be.

CHAPTER 2

The commotion in the park should have drawn Collin, the Earl of Frossly's, attention. It normally would have, but he had too much on his mind. He'd rode into the park more out of habit than because he had any desire to do so. His stallion blew out a breath and lifted his head as if nodding at a nearby horse. That amused him. Were the two exchanging some sort of greeting?

Collin pulled on the reins and brought his horse to a halt. His good friend, Cameron, the Duke of Partridgdon, came to a stop beside him. They had been riding together in communicable silence. Neither one of them had much to say and seemed to have found comfort in not having to carry a conversation. The duke had returned to England for a short trip. Cameron stayed out of the country more often than not—his way of avoiding the marriage his family had forced him to agree to. If he hadn't, the dukedom would have been in ruins. The betrothal had guaranteed early funds from the chit's dowry to sustain it. Cameron hated the contract and the idea of marrying a woman he'd been tied to for almost two decades. She'd been a mere child when the agreement had been signed.

Collin's situation didn't appear to be much better...

"What do you suppose that is all about?" Cameron broke the silence.

He shrugged. "I'm sure we don't wish to know. It is probably riddled with drama neither one of us particularly need to become embroiled with."

"You're probably correct," Cameron agreed. He narrowed his gaze and stared across the park. "The one chit looks familiar."

Collin turned to glance in the direction of the commotion. He didn't recognize the two ladies. He frowned. "Is the blonde chit wearing breeches?"

What had the lady been thinking? He could not ascertain one reason for a woman to dress so brazenly. Although, he had to admit he was rather curious about her now. Had that been her purpose?

Did she hope to attract a gentleman's attention? It was still not the correct way to behave. If she'd hoped to gain notice, she had certainly done so, but he doubted it would be the kind she wanted. She would attract every rakehell and scoundrel the *ton* boasted.

"She is," Cameron said. "Do you know them?"

He shook his head. "I try to stay out of polite society. My sister would probably recognize them. If she were here, I'd ask." His sister, Kaitlin, had been happily married to the Earl of Shelby more than fifteen years now. She had three children that kept her occupied…two sons, and a precocious daughter. "But as she isn't available, I do not dare to guess." He turned to Cameron. "Why, are you interested?"

Cameron frowned. "The other lady," he began. "Not the one in the breeches," he clarified. "She might be my fiancée."

"Ah," Collin said, suddenly understanding. "We should make haste then. Wouldn't do for her to realize you're in England, would it?"

"No," he agreed, then frowned again. "She's lovelier than I remember." The last bit was spoken in a mere murmur, but Collin had heard it, nonetheless.

Had this little outing given Cameron something

to consider? The dark-haired lady was indeed beautiful. At least what he could see of her. The blonde though...the daring one...something about her interested him. The fact that he could see every one of her curves outlined in those breeches certainly didn't leave much to the imagination either. She hadn't thought this scheme of hers through. Any red-blooded male would find her attributes appealing, and Collin was far from saintly.

"Oh, no," Collin said as the Duke and Duchess of Weston, along with the Marquess and Marchioness of Seabrook, strolled into the park. Only then did he realize exactly who the blonde chit was, or more importantly, who her parents were. "The commotion is about to take a turn for the worse."

Cameron lifted a brow. "I do not understand."

He gestured toward the front of the park. "I do believe the Marchioness of Seabrook is about to strangle her only daughter." Cameron glanced at the two couples then over to the two vixens causing the uproar.

"Ah," his friend said, and then grinned. "It might be worth it to sit back and witness the scene unravel." He shook his head. "Not sure if I want to risk it though. It's a pity we cannot stay."

"True," Collin agreed. "The Duchess of Weston

may prove to be the voice of reason. She is teaching some medicinal practices to my cousin, Marian, and she's not what one might consider a typical lady of the *ton*. She has more...progressive ideas."

Cameron sighed. "It's best we make haste. The *ton* is too busy gossiping over what's before them, and we can make a quick exit."

"Lead the way," Collin told him.

He'd much rather return to his Uncle Charles's, the Earl of Coventry's, house anyway. He had to discern the best way to handle his current situation. If Cameron hadn't shown up unexpectedly, he would have stayed in the study perusing the ledgers of his estate. His estate manager had up and quit, and from what he could tell, the man had left everything in ruins. He'd siphoned funds from the estate coffers and didn't do any of the repairs. Collin might have to go to Peacehaven and live at his manor until they were all done to his liking. He didn't trust leaving it to anyone else to complete.

Collin still had to talk to the authorities about tracking the man down. He hated that he'd lounged in London, living a mercurial life, while he'd been robbed blind. What a fool he'd been. He should have gone to his estate a long time ago. If there hadn't been so much pain involved regarding his ancestral home, he might have. He hadn't returned to Peacehaven since his parents's death. He wasn't certain he could go without his heart ripping into pieces, but it seemed he had little choice. No one else could do it for him, and it was time he grew up and stopped avoiding his responsibilities.

They exited the park without anyone noticing. Collin glanced back one last time at the lady in breeches. Part of him hoped they crossed paths again. He wanted to ask about her adventure and the reasoning. It would be an interesting tale... He would be unlikely to see her again though. Soon, he'd be in the country, buried in house repairs and farming updates. None of that would have anything to do with an unconventional lady that dared to ride her horse in the park in men's clothing...

CHARLOTTE PACED HER BEDROOM, WHERE SHE'D BEEN banished upon returning home. Once there, she'd stripped off the borrowed men's clothing and redressed herself in her own undergarments and gown. Her mother would have a fit if she came downstairs still wearing breeches. For a moment, she had thought her mother might throttle her in the park. She couldn't recall ever seeing the Marchioness of Seabrook that angry before. Her face had been so flushed it rivaled a bright red apple for coloring.

Her parents had been incredibly angry. Far more livid than she had anticipated... This scheme of hers had seemed like such a good way to get what she wanted. Now she questioned the veracity of what she had believed. She hated disappointing her parents. Especially her father...she'd always admired him and how brave he'd been during the war. If she ever married, she hoped the gentleman she gave her heart to could be equally as courageous. Not that she hoped the country experienced anything resembling a war again, but she still wanted the quality to be deep inside her fictitious love before she gave him her heart. It didn't seem like too much to ask...

The door to her bedchamber flung open. A maid stepped inside and curtsied. "Pardon me, milady," she said. "Your mother and father request your presence in the salon."

Her heart beat heavily in her chest. This was it. The reckoning she'd caused would gain her permission to travel back to Seabrook. She would have the freedom to work on her novel and not worry about any social engagements. Charlotte swallowed hard and took a fortifying breath. "Thank you, Mildred," she said to the maid. She was proud of how evenly she spoke. Her voice didn't show the nervousness that rattled through her entire body. It was a miracle she wasn't shaking uncontrollably. Somehow, she doubted *request* had been the tone her parents had used—more like ordered or demanded. *Request* implied she had a choice. Charlotte was pretty certain *demand* was the correct word to describe what her parent's desired of her.

She stopped outside of the salon and took another breath. Somehow, she thought she'd need it for the upcoming confrontation. Charlotte took a tentative step and then entered the salon. She kept her head held high. It wouldn't do her any good to show weakness. Her parents, as much as she loved them, were merciless. They'd have her weeping and running back to her room if she allowed them to gut her with their words. That wasn't to say they were unkind. Her parents had always been loving and nurturing as she grew from a child to a young woman, but they also didn't suffer fools. Charlotte would wager they considered her deeds beyond foolish.

Her mother looked serene without one strand of her midnight locks out of place. There wasn't much color in her complexion, only the hint of pink. Gone was the dark red blotches, and nothing but creamy skin remained.

"You wished to see me?" It wasn't really a question, but somehow it slipped out as one...

"Please have a seat," her father said gesturing to a chair near the settee they were already seated at. Her mother calmly poured a cup a tea and put two lumps of sugar in it. She then sipped it as if she wasn't about to deliver a punishment to her daughter. *Merciless...*

"We're not going to discuss your actions," her father began. His golden blond hair was disheveled. He must have run his hand through his locks several times in frustration. "It's pointless to repeat the details of the incident. What is done is done." He lifted a glass filled with amber liquid and took a sip. No tea for her father... That was brandy he had in his glass. She'd driven her dear father to drink. She wasn't certain how she felt about that. Perhaps she should be ashamed, and maybe she was, but she had achieved her goal so she would continue on this path if she hoped to see its complete fruition. "What we are going to discuss is what we have decided to do about the situation."

Her mother picked up a scone and slathered it

with jam and took a bite. Was she going to ignore Charlotte for the entirety of the conversation? Somehow, that hurt...worse. "I understand," she answered. Somehow, she managed to keep her tone void of emotion. So far, she was handling it all without issue. She could do this.

"Do you have anything to say for yourself?"

Charlotte shook her head slowly. It wouldn't do any good to defend her actions. She had dressed as a man and rode through Hyde Park...on purpose. There was no excuse that would be acceptable. "I don't wish to compound anything with any defense of my actions. I'll accept what you decide." There was only one place she would be sent. She prayed her little escapade in the park would not be for naught. They had to send her home. They just had to. Charlotte hated that she caused her parents any undo anxiety, but causing a scandal was the only sure way to guarantee they'd send her home. She would not change anything she'd done. It would give her what she wanted most...to return to Seabrook. For that she couldn't allow herself to feel guilty or back down from what she wanted. Her parents didn't understand what she wanted, and therefore, she had to make them do what she needed. Even if they were disappointed with her.

"That is wise of you," her father told her. "Especially as you don't have a choice."

That didn't sound...good. A foreboding settled deep inside her gut. "All right..." She swallowed hard. "What have you decided?"

"We had a couple of options," her father began. Couple? There was only one: Seabrook... What did he mean? "Seabrook is always an option, but if we sent you home, you wouldn't learn any profound lessons. So that won't do at all."

Her heart sank and her stomach started to hurt. What was happening? Where were they going to send her? This was wrong, all wrong. "If I'm not to go home, where will I go?" Had she done it for nothing? She never considered they might not send her to Seabrook. This...she had no words for how this made her feel. She had to remain strong. Maybe she could still accomplish her goals, even if it hadn't gone exactly as she had wanted it to.

A smile formed on her mother's face. It was almost...menacing. "I thought that was what you wanted." She set her tea down and met Charlotte's gaze. "You're going to stay with your Great Aunt Seraphina. She lives alone, and it'll be a benefit to her to have you with her for the next several months." Her mind went blank for a few moments as that information settled inside her mind. She was disappointed she wasn't going home, and they were sending her to a place she was bound to hate. They were punishing her, as she expected they would, but so thoroughly that she started to regret what she had done.

Aunt Seraphina...was ancient. All right, that was perhaps an exaggeration. Charlotte didn't want to spend the next several months with her aunt as company. She'd want to talk and have social engagements; all the things Charlotte wanted to avoid. This had not gone as planned, but she couldn't go back and change anything. She had done this to herself, and she'd have to make do with the situation. How bad could it be?

EXCERPT: NEVER DEFY A VIXEN

NEVERHARTTS BOOK ONE

DAWN BROWER

USA TODAY
BESTSELLING AUTHOR
Dawn
Brower
A
NEVERHARTTS
NOVELLA
Never
Defy
a
Vixen

PROLOGUE

*L*ightning flashed, and lit up the night sky, illuminating the room more than mere candlelight could. Thunder cracked, echoing through the silence permeating the room. Lady Wilhelmina Neverhartt, Billie to her family and friends, swallowed hard and took a step toward her mother's sickbed. Her father, Richard Neverhartt, the Earl of Seville hadn't survived the day, the illness overtook him hours earlier. Her mother, Augusta, the Countess of Seville seemed to be losing her battle and soon would join her husband in the ever after.

"Billie," her sister, Theodora—Teddy, whispered. "Don't go in there."

"I have to," she replied, but even she could hear

the dread in her voice. None of them wanted to witness their mother's last breath. Whatever illness their parents had brought back with them in their travels, seemed deadly, and the idea they might take ill too... Billie swallowed hard. She had to be strong. Soon she'd be responsible for herself, and her four siblings. Damon, the youngest of them all, at barely three and ten had inherited their father's title. Not that it did any of them much good because the estate had been rendered destitute. That was why their father had traveled to another country. He had become embroiled in some investment that promised him a windfall. Billie was damn near certain that her father had been expecting a far different outcome than the death of him and his wife. Instead he'd doomed them all. She turned to her sister and said with a firm tone, "Teddy, go make sure Carly and Chris don't come here. We can't all risk contracting this illness. Damon is asleep thank goodness."

The twins, Carolina and Christiana, were both headstrong, and had difficulties following instructions. Teddy was shy and kept to herself. She might not be able to convince them to remain in their bedchambers. Chris was more likely to do as she pleased, Carly might see reason.

"I'll try," Teddy said softly. "But you know how they are…" Her voice trailed off. She nibbled on her lower lip, her apprehension nearly spilling from her as she stared at the sickroom. "Do you really need to go in there?"

"I do," she insisted. "Now go handle our impetuous sisters." Billie couldn't deal with them all, and her mother's certain death. She needed Teddy to do this one thing for her.

Teddy nodded and turned away from Billie. She took another tentative step into the room as a flash of lightning guided her path. The crack of thunder that followed had her jumping even though she'd expected it. Slowly she creeped forward until she neared her mother's bedside. Her blonde hair looked almost as white as the pillow underneath her head. Her skin had lost all color, and her lips were dry and cracked. She took a shallow breath that almost crackled and wheezed with each squeeze of air into her lungs. Her cheeks had sunken in and become more pronounced with her weight loss. The woman lying in the bed was her mother, but she seized looking like the woman who had raised her days, no weeks ago.

"Mama," she said. The word was barely audible as

it passed her lips. Billie swallowed and tried again. "Mama," she said louder. "I'm here for you."

The countess's eyelids fluttered open and she turned toward Billie. Her mother's eyes were glazed over, almost unfocused as she stared at her. "Billie?"

"Yes, Mama," she said. Should she touch her? Put her hand in hers? Billie had no idea how to act around this frail creature that was her mother. She had no experience with death or illness. Billie was afraid to make the wrong move or make anything worse, if it could be worse, for her mother. "What..." Billie took a deep breath. "Tell me what you need."

"Come a little closer." Billie took another tentative step. There wasn't much distance now between her, and the countess. Maybe if she somehow detached herself from the sight before her she could endure it. At least for a little while... There were no more servants to help. They had all left as soon as they realize how sick the earl and countess were. None of them wanted to risk becoming ill, and well, they didn't have the funds to pay them. That chore had fallen to Billie, and it had drained every ounce of energy she could muster. She was ready to give up, but she'd already lost one parent, and she hoped there might be a chance to save her mother. By some miracle neither she, not her siblings had taken sick, but that didn't mean they wouldn't, they still could, and she prayed that fate wouldn't befall them.

Her mother moved her hand toward Billie. "I'm sorry we've been such a strain on you." Billie had chosen not to mention her father's death. That might prove too much for her mother to bear. She was already fighting as hard as she could. She didn't need to know that the earl had lost his battle. "I'm afraid that it will only become more difficult as the days pass." She wheezed in a breath. "I don't want to die." Her voice shook a little as she spoke. Tears threatened to fall, but Billie reined them in. She could cry later in the privacy of her room. "But death is here to claim me. I'm so, so sorry," she said. "I cannot say that enough, and nothing I say will make this better. He was foolish, your father, and I was even more so to follow him to that forsaken country. We're both paying that price now."

Billie was having more difficulty fighting those tears. "It's all right Mama."

"It isn't," she said. "But you're a dear for saying so. I wish we could have left you with something, anything, to aid you in the trying time to come. You don't need to tell me your father is no longer in this world. I felt him pass, and soon I'll join him."

"I'm sorry," she whispered. She never would have expected her mother to confess such a thing. Billie didn't even know that it was possible... "I didn't want to burden you with the truth."

Her lips tilted upward into a waning smile. She could barely keep them tilted upward and it hurt to witness that lack of strength. "You're a resilient, brave girl. You're going to need to be tougher than you have ever been, and fight for you, and your brother, and sisters. They're going to need you. I wish it could have been different. Go see the Duke of Graystone—he's your father's godfather, and he'll help you."

Not long after those words her mother took her last breath. A solitary tear rolled down Billie's cheek. She had a feeling that she wasn't going to like how the Duke of Graystone would assist them with their difficulties, but she had to gather all the fortitude she could, and handle it. That's what her mother expected her to do, and her siblings needed from her. She no longer could live her life for herself, and a part of her hated her parents for leaving her with so many complications to overcome. They were selfish, and she didn't have any room to be anything other than the dependable older sister. Her life was no longer her own, if it had ever been...

CHAPTER 1

One month later...

*B*illie stared at the ornate mahogany desk and frowned. She wanted to be anywhere than her current location. The Duke of Graystone had yet to join her, and she found it odd that his butler had shown her to what she presumed to be his grace's study. She *had* come to ask the duke for help, so perhaps somehow the butler had known that.

Where was he? She shuffled in her seat. The chair was hard and she couldn't find a comfortable position. Hopefully the duke wouldn't take much longer. Though she had to admit that she dreaded the upcoming conversation. Billie hated begging, but she didn't have much choice. If the duke refused to help them…

She swallowed hard. Billie couldn't think of that. The duke would help them. Her mother had told her to come to him, and she had put it off as long as possible. This was their last chance. The creditors had taken everything that hadn't been nailed down. They couldn't take the Seville estate because it was entailed, but they could no longer afford its upkeep. They had no way to feed themselves, or continue to afford the very basics of their needs.

Shuffling sounds echoed behind her. She turned toward the sound as an elderly man strolled into the room. He had white hair on the sides of his head and shiny bald top. His stomach protruded outward and hung low over his trousers. The buttons of his waistcoat looked like they might pop if he breathed too hard. He had a wooden cane in his left hand that scraped across the floor as he moved toward her.

"Hello, dear," he said. His voice was a little wispy as he spoke and she had to strain a little to hear him.

"Hello," she said demurely. Billie didn't know what else she should say. It seemed a little stupid, and repetitive. She cleared her throat. "That is…how are you your grace?" Not much better, but it would have to do.

"I'm fine." He shuffled his feet and scaped his cane across the floor as he moved to his seat behind the desk. Once he reached his chair he lowered himself slowly. It was painful to watch. After he was settled he turned his attention to her. "I was saddened to hear about your father's death. If I could have attended the funeral I would have. My health isn't what it once was."

She believed it. Witnessing his slow gait, Billie would swear she could almost hear his bones creak with each step he took. "It's all right, your grace, it was a small funeral." They couldn't even afford that much. If they would have been forced to have a larger one she'd have been at the duke's feet begging the same day. "It's best you not strain yourself. My father would have understood." Her father was selfish to the core and probably would have cursed the duke's neglect, but she wouldn't voice that sentiment.

The duke coughed. "You've been waiting awhile and I don't wish to keep you longer than necessary. What brings you by today?"

Billie wasn't certain if she was happy he decided to dispense with the social niceties or irritated he didn't wish to have a pleasant conversation with her. Though, on second thought, she didn't really wish to spend any more time in his company than necessary. There was a strange odor in the room she feared was coming from the duke considering she hadn't noticed it before he'd entered.

"Before my mother…" She took a deep, fortifying breath. "My mother said that if I needed help I should come to you." Billie prayed he didn't send her packing for boldly asking for charity. It hurt to have to come to him. If she could have found another way she would have.

"Did she?" He lifted a brow. "Augusta always did believe the best of me."

What did that mean? "My mother saw the good in everyone." Otherwise she never would have married Billie's father, or followed him wherever he went. She might still be alive if she had stayed home.

"That's true," the duke said. He leaned forward, placing his elbows on his desk, then steepled his fingers together. "Tell me, Lady Wilhelmina why should I help you?"

Billie should have expected that question, but it took her by surprise. She had no idea how to answer it. Her mother said the duke would help them. What if she'd been wrong? "My mother…"

"Doesn't know everything," the duke interrupted her. "She never should have assumed anything."

They were doomed. The duke would not help them. Tears threatened to fall but she held them back. This odious man would not reduce her to a crying ninny. "So you won't help me and my siblings? You'll let us starve?" or worse…

"I'm not responsible for you or your family. My obligation was to your father, what little it was, and with his death that obligation, in my opinion, ended."

He was an odious man. "I see." And she did. The duke's selfishness outweighed her fathers a thousandfold. "I'm sorry I've wasted your time." She stood and turned to head away from him.

"I never said I wouldn't help."

Billie stopped and turned toward him. "You as much said you wouldn't. Why would I believe otherwise?"

"We can come to an arrangement." He gestured toward the seat. "You have something I am very much in need of, and if you agree, I'll support the rest of that broad Oscar and Augusta spawned."

"What do you need from me?" Billie had a feeling, deep down, that she wasn't going to like what he had to say.

"Sit down," he ordered. "This is not something we should discuss with you hovering over me."

She was hardly doing any such thing. Billie wasn't even close to him; nonetheless, she did as he instructed and settled back into the uncomfortable chair. "Now that I've done as you asked, can you please explain what you meant."

"It's simple really," he began. "My scoundrel of a nephew is my heir, and I'd rather he not inherit my estate."

Billie's stomach plummeted at those words. "So you want me to…"

"Marry me and bear my son," he finished for her. "I can have a special license today, and we can consummate the marriage tonight. My late wife didn't fulfill her obligation, but I have no doubt you will do well. Your mother had five children. Surely you can manage one."

The last thing Billie wanted was to marry an old man, and the idea of letting him touch her… Her stomach rolled again. It would be awful. Somehow she would have to get through it though. This was the only way she could save her family. "All right." She agreed before she changed her mind and ran from the house screaming.

"Good." He grinned. "You and I are going to have a lot of fun together."

Billie doubted that very much…

***

The wedding was scheduled to take place in less than an hour. Billie was close to losing what little contents were inside her stomach.

"Don't do this," Teddy said. "We'll find another way."

"There is no other way," Billie said firmly. "I have to. This way you, Carly, and Chris can make fabulous matches. Damon will be able to go to Eton." She pasted a smile on her face. "That's worth any price I have to pay, and at least I'll be a duchess." She would not think about the wedding night. The duke would surely crush her in his efforts to beget a child on her.

"Maybe you'll get lucky and the old duke will croak soon," Carly said.

"That would be a blessing," Chris said and looked at Billie. "What are the chances of that happening."

"Not before I have to suffer through the consummation," she said dryly. "My luck is not that good."

The twins laughed. "At least you still have a sense of humor. You're going to need it married to that old goat," Chris said. "I really wish you didn't have to do this."

So did Billie. "There's no other choice." Her stomach rumbled. She might vomit yet… "We will all be fine." And the duke *was* old. She might be able to have a second marriage built on love not necessity. "I promise that none of you will have to make this sort of sacrifice."

Teddy stepped forward and wrapped her arms around Billie. "I love you and I want to make this right for you. Please don't do this. I want you to be happy, and you'll never be happy married to an old man that only wants to use you." Her voice wobbled a little as she spoke. Clearly she was fighting tears.

"You're right," she said as she hugged her sister tight. "I won't be happy as his wife. At least not in the way you are suggesting. What will make me happy is knowing my sisters, and my brother, are safe and cared for. I can make that happen. I weighed the cost and consider it worth taking. Don't be sad for me."

"I can't help it," Teddy replied. She took a step back and wiped the tears from her eyes.

A knock echoed through the room. "The vicar is here and ready to perform the ceremony," the butler said. "If you'll follow me I'll show you to the salon. His grace doesn't like to be left waiting."

But he had no problem making other's wait... Billie didn't say that part aloud though. She nodded and followed the butler with her sisters trailing behind her. Soon she'd say vows to honor and obey a man she barely knew a thing about. He'd have power over her and would use it to his advantage. She hated the very thought of giving herself to him. Part of her didn't believe in love, at least not for herself. Maybe this was for the best. Perhaps she should make a vow to herself...never to fall in love, and never to allow a man into her heart who would make her want to throw caution to the wind. She would not make her mother's mistake.

There was no decorations or indication a wedding was going to be held in the salon. The duke stood next to a much younger man, but still older than Billie. If she were to guess the vicar was closer to her father's age. The duke was easily three decades older, probably more, than her father.

"Good," the duke said. "You're here. Now we can begin." He gestured for Billie to join them."

The wedding went by in a blur. Probably because Billie didn't want to recall one second of it. She was signing her life away and afterward nothing would ever be the same again. "I now pronounce you man and wife," the vicar said. "May the lord bless your marriage for many years to come."

Billie hoped not. If possible she hoped her part of this marriage would be over with in the first year and she didn't have to endure the duke's attention after that. Though he might want to try for a spare. Lord help her if he did...

"Now that the formalities are done with," the duke began. "It's time for the fun part. I'll meet you in your bedchamber."

"This soon?"

"It's nighttime," the duke said. "No reason to wait."

She swallowed hard and followed a maid to her chamber. Billie lost all ability to think as the maid helped her undress. When her gown was removed and Billie stood alone in only her shift the duke entered the room. He wore a robe that barely fit around his robust waist. "Leave," he ordered the maid. He reached for Billie. "Let me see what I paid for." His breathing was heavy and harsh as he moved toward her. With each step he took his face became redder and redder, with his cheeks the most flushed.

She wanted to step back but knew she couldn't. Billie closed her eyes and prepared for his groping.

She could do this. She could…and if she kept telling herself that perhaps she would make it to the end in one piece.

He gasped and then a loud thump filled the room. Billie opened her eyes and stared down at the duke laying on the ground. His face had lost all color, which was unbelievable considering how bright red it had been mere moments ago, and he didn't look as if…he was breathing. "Your Grace?" Her voice cracked as she spoke those two words.

He didn't answer. Billie leaned down and checked. Oh God…he was dead. What the hell was she going to do now?

Order Here: https://books2read.com/NeverDefyaVixen

EXCERPT: WHEN AN EARL TURNS WICKED

BLUESTOCKINGS DEFYING ROGUES 1

DAWN BROWER

USA TODAY
BESTSELLING AUTHOR

Dawn Brower

When an Earl Turns Wicked

PROLOGUE

Southington Castle, England, 1808

The day was like any other one in England. Rainfall had become a normal enough occurrence that Jonas didn't notice it—even as it dripped down his face, drenching him completely. He stared at the chiseled stones in the cemetery near Southington's chapel. Only members of his family were buried there—many he never met personally. Pictures of them filled the great hall, but they were history to him, and he'd been able to distance himself from their stories. This, however, was far different.

His life would never be the same. The death of his father had marked an unchangeable truth. The duke now had control over Jonas's life. His grandfather was a tyrant and had always attempted to browbeat his will into him. His father had been the one person he'd been able to count on. A buffer the duke couldn't break through, and he'd tried often.

So, no, the cold didn't matter because he was numb through and through. Rain? Paltry in comparison to what he had yet to face. The Duke of Southington, his grandfather, hadn't started yet—mainly because he couldn't. There were people around, and he dared not cause a scene. Once all the mourners departed, things would start to unravel ever further around him. Would his grandfather allow him to return to Eton? What about his mother? Would she have it in her to fight him? Somehow, he doubted everything and yet prayed for anything resembling his life before his father's death.

"Lord Harrington," a man said as he rested his hand on Jonas's shoulder. How could *he* be the earl now? That was his father's name, and he doubted he'd ever become accustomed to it. "It's time to head back."

He glanced up at the man as the rain continued to drip down his face. His hair was black, but had already started to turn to gray along the sides. Jonas barely knew him, but Lord Coventry had been a friend of his father's. "I'm not ready," he told him.

"George was a good man," Lord Coventry said. "He loved you."

"I know," Jonas replied woodenly. He'd long ago stopped feeling and now went through the motions. What else could he do? Lord Coventry was correct— it was long past time to go, yet he couldn't move. Once he left, it would all become too real for him. His grandfather would start barking orders, and he had years before he could be free of him. Three long years to be exact—once he turned eighteen he could seize control of his inheritance. As long as his grandfather didn't find a way to break the will. "But that doesn't change anything."

"No," Lord Coventry agreed. "He's still gone, and nothing will ever bring him back."

If Jonas were capable of crying, he'd have done so days ago. It was probably a good thing he hadn't. Any sign of weakness would have set his grandfather off. He had to be brave, and somehow find the strength to move on sooner than he'd like. His father deserved to be mourned, but he'd understand why Jonas couldn't openly do it. "I'm ready now." Jonas didn't look at Lord Coventry. He spun on his heels and began the long trek back to Southington Castle.

He hated his grandfather's home—it was as cold as he was. There wasn't anything welcoming about it.

"Lord Harrington—"

"Don't call me that," Jonas interrupted. The sound of his father's title shot pain through his already aching heart. He didn't want to think or feel. Everything reminded him of his father and the loss that he couldn't escape. The title... That was more than he could bear.

Lord Coventry cleared his throat. "It's who you are now."

"That may be." Jonas swallowed hard. "But filling my father's shoes is something I'm not yet prepared for. I can't hear his title without thinking of him and what I've lost."

"I understand," Coventry said and sighed. "You're too young to have lost your father already. If I had a son..." He shook his head. "That doesn't matter. You have a long road ahead of you, and there's probably no one you feel you can trust. You might not know it yet, but you can trust me." He paused for a moment before continuing, "What would you like me to call you?"

"Nothing," Jonas said. "I doubt we will see each other again after today."

The older man laughed. It was a foreign sound,

considering their surroundings. Sadness permeated everything around them, yet the earl had found something humorous. Coventry seemed like a likeable sort and in another time, Jonas may have liked him. Somehow, he doubted he'd find anything appealing or even joyous for a long time.

Coventry gestured toward the castle in the distance. "We shall see. Come, let's get out of this rain."

The earl followed behind Jonas as they entered the castle. He didn't stay long after that. He'd spoken to the duke quietly before his departure, and the duke didn't argue or order the earl around. That alone made Jonas wonder what they'd discussed.

"Now that everyone is gone we have some things to discuss, boy." His grandfather stormed across the room and glared down at him. "Starting with your education... I was going to keep you here, but Coventry made a good point. You'll need to make connections, and those are rooted in school. So, I'll allow you to return to Eton—at least for the rest of this school year. We'll revisit that idea before the next term."

He owed the earl far more than he realized. Never had he truly believed his grandfather would allow him to return to school. "Thank you."

"Don't thank me yet," his grandfather said gruffly. "We have a lot of work ahead of us to prepare you for the dukedom."

He was barely an earl, and now he had to worry about grandfather's title? The Southington title was no longer entailed, but he wouldn't remind the duke of that. Jonas wanted to curl up into a ball and sleep for days—no, weeks. That was the cowardly way though, and he refused to give in to it. "Where is Mother?"

"She's gone to live with her sister," he replied. "Your mother is too delicate for Southington. Don't worry. Your father made sure she'd be provided for."

His mother had abandoned him? He'd always been closer to his father, but still... She left him alone with the duke, and she was well aware of his brutish nature. He had no problems using his fists to make a point. The Harrington title was prestigious, but he wouldn't have control of the estate for many years. They had plenty of funds as long as they did what the duke wanted. His father had decided to cut as many ties as possible with Southington. They lived in a small townhouse in London, and his father had invested in a profitable shipping company with the income he had available. They didn't live in splendor, but they'd been comfortable.

None of it had made the duke happy, but then nothing could. He liked having control over his family, and losing it had made him cut them out of his life. That was until his father died and he saw a way to wiggle his way back in. Now, Jonas was his ward until he gained full access to his inheritance. It was not a huge sum, but it would be enough for him to break free.

"May I be excused?" The duke hit Jonas's mouth with his fist before he was fully prepared for its impact. Jonas jerked backward involuntarily, but then gained control as quick as possible. He lifted his gaze and stared the duke in the eye, repeating his request, "May I be excused now?" Leaving without permission would prolong the torture, and he didn't want another punch to the face, or anywhere else.

The duke nodded, and Jonas left as fast as his feet would carry him. He didn't run as he wanted to because he would not give in to the duke's bullying. If he darted out of the room, his grandfather would find a reason to make him stay. Instead, he walked briskly and steadily until he reached his chambers. Only then, once the door was closed and he had privacy, did he give in to the emotions raging through him. The tears he'd held in finally flowed freely, and he grieved for his father.

LONDON, 1812

Jonas picked up the glass of brandy on the table and took a drink. He set it back down and stared at the cards in his hand. So far, luck hadn't been on his side, and he was steadily losing what funds he had. He should have given up a long time ago but stupidly thought he'd win if he kept playing. Freedom had led him astray when it should have brought him happiness. He learned fast that the latter was an elusive emotion not meant for him.

"I think it's time to call it a night," announced Jason Thompson, Earl of Asthey. He ran his fingers through his dark blond hair and grinned like a cat that'd caught the prize mouse. "It's been a productive night."

At least it was going well for one of them. "I'm ready too." He threw his cards on the table. "I've lost too much as it is." And he had very little he could afford to lose. His grandfather still held onto most of the purse strings. Somehow, the duke had found a way to gain control over a large part of his inheritance. Jonas had won his independence a year ago, but he wasn't truly free. The one thing he had left that the duke couldn't touch was a tiny sum his maternal grandmother had left him. It barely gave him enough to live on. He needed to figure out how to raise his income, but he was at a loss on how.

"That's a shame," Asthey said. "Winning big would solve a lot of your woes."

Jonas rolled his eyes. "I need more than I'd win in a few hands of cards to solve all that." It might help if his grandfather decided to roll over and die, but no, that wouldn't happen. The old man was too bullheaded to do anything as congenial as save the world from his type of meanness. "Where is Shelby?" Gregory Cain, the Earl of Shelby, was the other member of their trio. Jonas scanned the room for Shelby's midnight locks. They were his trademark. No one else had hair quite as sinfully dark as his. His friend was nowhere to be seen in the gaming hell.

"He found a light-skirt to his liking and appropriated a room for a bit of sport."

Of course he did... Shelby was quite the rake, and relished in ravishing any willing female in his vicinity. "Should we wait?"

"He knows his way home," Asthey replied. "I rather not wait on him to finish. He might take all night, or he could come out in an hour. It's hard to say with him."

"You're right," Jonas agreed. He stood and pulled

on his jacket and buttoned it over his waistcoat. "I'm tired and would rather sleep in my own bed."

They both headed to the front door and exited the gaming hell. It was still quite dark, and for once it was a rather clear night in London. The rain had been dreadful for days. The streets were filled with puddles and mud. They walked in silence for a few moments as they headed for a nearby hackney. As they stepped onto the road to cross over to the carriage, Jonas was yanked backward. He fell to the ground, his head smacking against the hard surface.

"Bloody hell," he said with a groan. "Why'd you do that?"

"I have a message for you." A big, burly man loomed over Jonas.

Jonas lifted a brow. "You might want to work on your delivery. I won't be recommending your service to anyone."

"Don't need it," the burly man replied. Jonas couldn't make out his features in the dark, but felt the sting of a fist hitting his jaw. "The message isn't the verbal kind."

The ruffian was poised to throw another punch, but was jerked backward before he could land it. The man hit the ground in much the same manner as Jonas had. Served the bastard right... Jonas leapt to his feet before the other man could get up. He rubbed his hand over his sore jaw. "Took you long enough." He turned to whom he'd thought was Asthey, but was shocked to find Lord Coventry instead.

"Where's Asthey?"

"There." Coventry pointed in the distance. He was battling a ruffian of his own. He landed a solid blow, and the man fell to the ground. "What is going on?"

"Unfortunately, this is the work of your grandfather," he replied. A hint of sadness echoed through his voice. "I heard a rumor and came to investigate the veracity of it."

"And?" Jonas didn't like where this conversation was going. His grandfather could do a lot of damage if he wanted to, and it appeared as if he'd decided to employ his power. He had to have all the information Coventry possessed so he could form a plan of his own. His grandfather's contacts were extensive and his reach even farther. In order to beat him at his own game Jonas might have to fight dirty.

"I'm afraid it was correct by the looks of things," Coventry answered.

Asthey joined them, shaking his hand in the air as he walked. "That hurts more than I want to admit. I might need to learn a thing or two about throwing a proper punch."

Coventry nodded. "I might be able to help you both." He turned to Asthey. "Go inside and fetch your friend, Shelby. I have a proposition for you all."

Asthey didn't question Coventry's order. He nodded and headed back into the gaming hell. Jonas watched him until he disappeared inside, and then turned back to Coventry. "What do you know?"

"Far more than you do," he replied cryptically. "The duke has plans for you, and he's not happy with your reluctance to follow them."

"That's something I know far too well." He wished the old man would leave him alone already. "Was this his way of forcing me to go to Southington?"

"I'm not entirely sure what he hoped to accomplish tonight," Coventry admitted. "I know he arranged it, and I'm here to help if you'll allow it."

Jonas was so tired of constantly fighting with his grandfather. There had to be a way to stop him from coming after him again and again. "What do you have in mind?"

Asthey and Shelby came out of the gaming hell and joined them. Shelby carried his cravat in his hand and was straightening his jacket. "This better be important," Shelby muttered. "The chit was..."

"We don't need to know," Asthey said, interrupting him.

Coventry smiled. "I believe you boys will fit right in."

"I don't follow," Jonas said, then frowned. "Fit in where?"

"A very special club," he replied. "Come along. I'll explain everything and how it'll help you with Southington, your social life, and even financially, if you like."

He didn't understand how a club could do all that, but he was willing to hear Coventry out. He had saved him from being beaten, and as long as Jonas had his two friends with him, he didn't see the harm. They could decide together if it was something worth doing. They'd stuck together this long.

They followed Coventry to a nearby carriage and climbed inside. It rolled across the cobbled street with ease. The interior was plush, and the seats rather comfortable. Jonas had never ridden in a carriage so fine. After a short drive, the carriage stopped. They all got outside to find an elegant townhouse with a W emblazoned near the door.

Where were they? What had Coventry said earlier? Something about a club.

"Where are we?" Asthey asked vocalizing Jonas's thoughts.

"Doesn't look like much," Shelby replied. "Why'd I leave that lovely lass again?

Coventry pulled a key out of his pocket that had the same W on the top of it. He pushed it into the lock and opened the door." "Gentleman, please come inside." He led them from the foyer into the main part of the house.

The outside expertly disguised the decadence found inside. Rich velvet draped the windows. The settees, chaise lounge, and every chair in the place had similar color scheme of dark red and burnished brown. To the side was a long cherry banister that wound around an elaborate staircase. To the side was a large room with a blazing fireplace. Several men sat at one of the tables as they played cards. Each one had a beautiful, scantily clad woman on their lap. Jonas's mouth fell open at everything he saw, and he couldn't believe he didn't know the place existed. He turned to Coventry and said, "You have our attention. Want to explain this to us now?" He continued to stare at the luxuriousness of his surroundings.

Coventry smiled. "Welcome to the Coventry Club. You have been nominated for admission—if you want to join. There are rules, of course," Coventry told them. "Nothing too extreme, but you should all find them reasonable. Keep the club a secret, and you forfeit your membership once you marry—only the leader of the group is allowed to have a wife and retain his membership. If you're wondering who that is—I am the one currently in charge of the club and its members." He glanced at each one of them and asked, "Do you wish to be a part of all this?" He held his arms out wide.

They all nodded immediately. Jonas didn't give it much thought, and figured the other two hadn't either. The sheer excess of the place had won them over. The rest he could figure out later.

It was a decision he never regretted...

CHAPTER 1

London, 1823

*D*ark gray clouds floated in the sky above, threatening to unleash rain upon everyone who dared to walk the streets of London. Lady Marian Lindsay stared up at them as she chewed her bottom lip. It was not a good sign, and she hoped the bad omen didn't lead to a disastrous meeting with Sir Anthony Davis. Not that rain wasn't commonplace in England—because it most certainly graced the country with regularity; however, Marian's luck never held when it deigned to fall from the sky. So her meeting with Sir Anthony would surely be doomed.

Nonetheless, she fully intended to go through with it. She had plans, and Sir Anthony stood in the way of them. Without his permission, she'd never become a part of the Royal Medical Society. They had this misbegotten notion medicine and women didn't mix. She hoped to change his mind and have him recommend her for admission.

She'd been studying medicine and herbs her entire life. All right, maybe not that long, but it felt like it. Her interest started almost a decade ago after her aunt and uncle's death. They'd both been in a terrible carriage accident near her family estate. Her father was the Earl of Coventry. Her uncle, the Earl of Frossly, married her Aunt Belinda and became a part of the family. After their death, Marian's mother had been desperate with grief and the loss of her beloved younger sister.

Everything in Marian's life changed after that. Her two cousins came to live with them, and her mother became sick following their arrival—leaving her launch into society, as well as her cousin's, forgotten. Not that she had minded especially once her mother succumbed to her illness and they lost her forever. Her grief had been too great, and she'd decided she wanted more in life. Marian didn't want to marry and have children. She had much loftier goals—like becoming an actual physician and making a living helping people.

Which brought her back to Sir Anthony—he had to let her into the society. This was the next step to gaining the knowledge she needed to become a doctor. She glanced up at the sky once more.

"Please hold off until I'm done," she begged. "I need a little bit of time." She quickened her pace until she reached Sir Anthony's building and pushed the door open. Marian entered as the rain started to fall. It pounded against the street, creating puddles almost instantly. She shut the door and blew out a relieved breath.

Someone cleared their throat. She turned and found two men standing inside, staring at her with a modicum of surprise etched on their faces. The older gentleman must have been Sir Anthony. He had dark hair streaked with gray. The other gentleman was rather handsome—dashing even. He had dark hair and devilish blue eyes. Much to her chagrin, she'd always found him enticing, and not because he was the most gorgeous male she'd ever seen. There was something about him that made the heart inside her chest beat heavily. Marian's whole body hummed with some unnamable energy. Jonas Parker, the esteemable Earl of Harrington, would always put her at a disadvantage, and sometimes she believed he knew it too. *Damn him.* "Hello, my lord," Marian greeted him and then turned to the older man. "Sir Anthony." She hoped her presumption was correct and he was the man she thought, or wouldn't that be embarrassing...

"Lady Marian," Lord Harrington said in a slow drawl. "Does your father know you're in this part of town?"

Drat. Of course that would be the first thing he'd ask—at least he hadn't corrected her about Sir Anthony. "My father is well aware of my activities." That wasn't entirely a lie. He did know she hoped to be a doctor and humored her. He didn't really believe she'd succeed, but she planned on proving him wrong. Men had all the advantages in society and women were given little say in their lives. Something she hated to the depths of her soul. "You needn't worry about me."

"What may we assist you with?" Sir Anthony asked. "Did the rain drive you inside?"

Lord Harrington lifted a brow. "I don't think that's it at all." He kept his gaze on Marian, unnerving her. He saw too much, and she rather disliked the scrutiny. "You're here because of your little project, aren't you?"

Anyone acquainted with her father, and therefore her, was aware of her desire to be a doctor. Her father boasted of her hobby even though he doubted her. It was his way of giving her his support. Not that it was a lot or even a stamp of approval, but it had managed to aid her in her quest thus far. "What if I am?" She jutted out her chin. "You aim to prevent me from taking the next step?"

He held out his hands in front of him. "Far be it from me to step in front of a bluestocking on a mission. By all means, say your piece and see if Sir Anthony is willing to assist you."

Sir Anthony glanced back and forth between them, but Marian barely noticed. She was irritated more than she should be. Lord Harrington was being nice by allowing her to speak—a sardonic, arrogant, and presumptuous...*man*. Rolling her eyes would not help her convince Sir Anthony she should be a part of the Royal Medical Society. She took a deep breath to calm herself. Calling him names inside her head would not further her goals. She had to pull herself together and try to present herself in the best light to Sir Anthony.

"You require something from me?" Anthony asked as he gave her his full attention. "What is it?"

"Well," she started. This was much harder than she thought it would be. "I have a request I hope you'll agree to."

"Oh?"

That was it. Nothing else from him or any encouragement for her to go on. Lord Harrington, the rogue, leaned against a nearby table and crossed his arms over his chest. He had a wicked grin on his too handsome face. If Marian wasn't a lady, she'd do something to wipe that knowing smile away. Someone should put him in his place, and maybe then he wouldn't be so condescending.

"I've been studying for a while to be a physician..."

"You have?" Sir Anthony scrunched his eyebrows together. "Your father knows you're doing this?"

"Well, yes," she said. "I did mention he was aware of my activities..."

"She's a bluestocking," Lord Harrington added. "You know how they are when they get an idea in their head. It's why I didn't stop her when she came in, if you'll recall."

Marian gave in and rolled her eyes. She couldn't help herself any longer. Why did she have to be attracted to him? He drove her mad in more ways than she could count, yet he was the one man her body became alive near. She hated him for it. "Thank you, my lord." She pasted a cheerful smile on her face. "You give glowing recommendations."

"It's the least I can do," he replied with that sinful voice of his. It sent shivers down her spine. "As you can see, Sir Anthony is quite scandalized with your chosen hobby. He's gone mute with the shock of it."

Damn him, he was right. Sir Anthony stared at her as if she were a bug to be studied in length. He hadn't said a word in several heartbeats. "I had hoped you'd foster my admission into the Royal—"

"Absolutely not," he responded with vehemence. "Ladies do not become doctors or study anything. I don't understand this generation and their need to poke their noses in things they best not be a part of."

"Some ladies find science and knowledge enticing," Marian said as she lifted her head in defiance. "Intelligence is quite an attractive asset to inspire to."

"Touché," Lord Harrington agreed. "But I'd take it a step further and suggest there are things a gentleman finds more attractive in a lady than what's inside their head."

She shook her head. "I didn't come here to debate

the qualities one looks for in a potential spouse. I want to become an active member of the Royal Medical Society."

"That's not going to happen, my dear. I'm afraid women are not allowed and never will be." Sir Anthony squared his shoulders, preparing for battle. Good, she planned on giving him something to fight about.

"Never is a long time to adhere to," Lady Marian replied. "Do you want to limit yourself when there are infinite possibilities if you'd open yourself up to them?"

"It's not up to me," Sir Anthony told her. "Society has rules for a reason. Go home and do something more ladylike. It truly is for the best."

She narrowed her gaze and pursed her lips together. *Ladylike?* He was much worse than Lord Harrington. At least the earl pretended to give her the space to argue her stance. Sir Anthony was an old-fashioned sycophant. He thought playing up to her feminine tributes would make her abandon her calling and do a bit of embroidery instead. Why could a man do anything he wanted, but a woman had inadequate options? If she decided to take up water colors or the pianoforte, they'd encourage her.

Being a doctor though? That was a ridiculous notion.

"Thank you for your sage advice," Marian replied with false sweetness. "I'll leave you gentleman to whatever you were discussing. It's time for me to return home. Good day." She curtsied and turned to the door.

"Wait," Lord Harrington demanded as he stepped forward. "I'll escort you."

"There's no need," she explained. Marian did not want him following her home. If he spoke to her father, then much more than a failed attempt to gain entry into the Royal Medical Society would befall her. "I managed to arrive here safely without an escort. I don't need one to see I find my way home."

"Perhaps," he replied cordially. "But I will be by your side every step of the way regardless. I'd never forgive myself if something happened to you and I could have prevented it." The corner of his mouth lifted enticingly. "I admire your father, and for that alone I'd see you safely to the ends of the Earth. Nothing you can say will talk me out of this."

Damn him. She cursed him for the thousandth time in the space of a half hour. At that rate, she'd start saying it aloud. There was no way she'd win in an argument with him. The easiest way would be to agree, but that irritated her nonetheless.

"Fine," she replied. "Have it your way."

"I always do," he retorted. "Good of you to see that." His blue eyes practically twinkled with mischief. He was a conceited scoundrel.

She ground her teeth together and refrained from responding. Instead, she spun on her heels and exited the building and Sir Anthony's misogyny. She would not give up on her dream. There had to be another way, and if there was, she'd find it.

The rain hadn't stopped while she was inside the shop. It beat against her in a rapid staccato, making her wish she'd stayed inside a bit longer, or procured a carriage. Why hadn't she planned this a little better? Because that would have made sense... She'd been blinded by her ambition and the need to be a part of something much bigger than herself. One day she'd learn the benefit of a well laid plan. Unfortunately, that day was not this one.

"Come with me," Lord Harrington leaned down and spoke directly into her ear. His heat enveloped her, making her forget where she was for a moment. He picked up her hand and rested it on his arm to lead her in the direction of his choosing. "My carriage is around the corner."

She blinked several times as rain continued to drown out the sound of the London Street. What was happening to her? She shook her head and did as Lord Harrington said. A carriage in this kind of weather was desirable, and for the first time since she saw him inside Sir Anthony's place, she was happy to have him near.

Thankfully, Lord Harrington's carriage wasn't far away. He helped her inside, but unfortunately, she was already soaked through. She couldn't wait to return home and put some distance between them. Uncomfortable wasn't a strong enough word to describe how he made her feel, and it didn't help that she was drenched from head to toe. She had to look a fright... What nonsense.

Why did she care if she looked less than desirable? Lord Harrington wasn't a potential suitor even if she was looking for a husband. He was one of the biggest rogues of the ton, and she was firmly on the shelf. Marian was a bluestocking and a spinster in the making, as untouchable as possible and quite content with that fate. Her pent up wantonness could dwindle down to nothing. She didn't need a man to find happiness.

Maybe she'd found a spot of luck in a sea of bad fortune. So, she'd taken a couple steps backward from her main goal. That didn't mean she couldn't find a way to move forward. For now, she'd allow Lord Harrington to see her home, and then she'd meet with her two closest friends to make a new plan. This was not the end of anything. Marian chose to see to it as a beginning. The likes of Sir Anthony and Lord Harrington would not discourage her.

www.ingramcontent.com/pod-product-compliance
Lightning Source LLC
Chambersburg PA
CBHW022115170626
46808CB00002B/735